THE TALL UNCUT

Books by Pete Fromm

The Tall Uncut

Indian Creek Chronicles

King of the Mountain

Monkey Tag

Dry Rain

Blood Knot

The
Tall
Uncut

LIVES AMID THE LANDSCAPES
OF THE AMERICAN WEST

STORIES BY PETE FROMM

THE LYONS PRESS

Printed in the United States of America

10 9 8 7 6 5 4 3 2 1

Design and typography by Jim Cook

Library of Congress Cataloging-in-Publication Data
Fromm, Pete.
    The tall uncut: lives amid the landscapes of the American West /
Pete Fromm.
        p.   cm.
    ISBN 1-55821-746-0
    1. Montana—Social life and customs—Fiction. 2. Outdoor
life—Montana—Fiction. I. Title.
PS3556.R5942T35   1998
813' .54—dc21   98-26098
                                                                      CIP

The Tall Uncut

ACKNOWLEDGEMENTS

"Mighty Mouse and Blue Cheese from the Moon" was first published in *Gray's Sporting Journal,* May 1990. "Bean Time" was first published in *Crosscurrents,* July 1991. "Spring" was first published in *Gray's Sporting Journal,* July 1991. "Self Inflicted" was first published in *The Double-Gun Journal,* February 1990. "Trash Fish" was first published in *Louisiana Literature,* December 1989. "Eulogy" was first published in *Alabama Literary Review,* May 1991. "Jump Shooting" was first published in *Gray's Sporting Journal,* September 1991. "Bone Yard" was first published in *Crosscurrents,* February 1991.

To Rose,
without whom none of this
would make much difference.

Mighty Mouse and
Blue Cheese from the Moon

I wasted the whole drive in to see her. It's a three hour trip, through the mountains at first, along the river, where I try to pick out fishing holes as I drive. Then the road passes the first swampy, beaver-clotted pools of the river and climbs along a single, miniscule feeder creek to the divide. After that it's hard to remember the timber and the dark curves of the canyons because you're into the high plains. They roll wildly, but smoothly, with any rough edges burred off by the incessant wind, and they seem to go on forever. But I missed it all with my daydreaming. I was too anxious to see her and to be alone with her on the river.

Like a fool, the first thing I asked was if she was ready to go. We stood there in the living room, holding each other. We were laughing about something, I can't remember what, when I asked. She didn't answer right away so I told her how the night would be. "There's a storm billowing up in the south," I said, letting her go to swing my arms to show the size of the clouds. "But it's clear all around them."

I was trying to get her excited, but as she let me go, it seemed that she might have had other plans for the evening.

"We'll float right on the edge of it, with the sky going that deeper blue and the first flecks of stars coming out, with the blackness taking up more and more in the thunderheads. And maybe the temperature will plunge twenty degrees or so, the way it can in summer."

She said, "That'd be nice," and she smiled. She wasn't excited about having to drive fifty miles by herself just to run the shuttle, but she smiled about that too, saying I was a hopeless romantic to want to drive all the way to Great Falls to see her through my rearview mirror for fifty miles.

She got her stuff together and we drove out, bumper to bumper on the pretty much deserted interstate. I bucked around with the canoe catching the wind and she waved whenever she caught me watching her in the mirror. I pointed out a coyote, then a group of pelicans that wheeled over the river by Cascade, flashing white when their backs caught the sun, then disappearing when they turned away. Like a flying wing of signal mirrors. When I looked to see if she'd seen them she had both hands clasped above her head waving them from side to side in an old time boxer's victory salute. Like Mighty Mouse used to do.

We left her truck at Craig then drove together the last five miles, babbling like high school dates. It'd been a long time since then, but after finally getting married we'd only gone a month before my "little" out of town job came up. That was six months ago and now I was only seeing her every other weekend. So we went on and on for the five minutes, talking of nothing in particular.

We got the canoe in and loaded and Mary zipped herself into a fishing vest—she doesn't fish but she's not much for swimming either. The storm had come up a lot faster than I expected and she pointed at the thunderheads, her hair pulling around to the wind, and rolled her eyes and stepped into the bow. We'd formed the habit, years ago, when she was just learning to canoe, of my always taking the stern, where you steer from, you know. Now, though she could pilot as well as I could, she did it from the front. I fished from the stern. Didn't make much sense, but that's how we did things.

"So where's dinner?" she said, paddling, without turning around, before I'd even set up a rod. It was an old joke—we hardly ever keep fish, and I laughed the way you do at old jokes when they remind you of all the other times you've heard them.

I'm not up on fishing the way some people are. I mean, I found my fly rods on the bottom of this very stretch of river. I've floated all my life, and swum, and done some fishing too, but I don't know about barometric pressure, or pH, or all that other high tech fishing mumbo-jumbo. Anyway, there was nothing rising, so I set up the rod with the sinking line and tied on a big, black, weighted nymph. I think it was a hellgrammite, but wouldn't want to have to bet on that. I found the fly box too, but not on the Missouri.

A rip of thunder let go, closer than I'd have guessed and it startled a gasp out of me. Mary really laughed at that, waving her paddle above her head.

I turned to shoot the clouds a look and you wouldn't've believed how close they were. And coming on like nobody's business. Mary caught me at that too. "We're going to get schmeered," she said. "I love it when you take me on dates."

We were a couple miles into the float, just before the wind really went crazy, carrying rain with it, when I finally hooked into something besides all those false little tugs the bottom gives out.

I could feel the fish was small, but hooked solid, so I was puffing and pulling, grunting things like "water on the reel," whenever the fish would make a run to click out a few feet of line.

It even broke the surface once, not jumped really, broached was more like it, and I hollered, "Tie me in." Then, as I was crying, "Nantucket sleighride!" she caught a good look at the fish. It was a whitefish, which was what I was beginning to suspect, and she chanted "Snout-trout, snout-trout," until the rain let loose.

There was the usual scramble for rain gear that we always put off too long. For some reason she was laughing so hard you couldn't tell if she was squeezing out tears or if it was just the rain.

I got pretty wet before getting the gear on because I had to unhook the whitefish. But when that rain let go, it let go. Usually the wind goes berserk before one of these storms gets on top of you, then dies out when the rain takes over. But this one just kept howling. I ruddered with my paddle and we were like a speedboat, driving downstream before the wind.

We were both laughing then. The lightning was blasting the cliffs, the thunder right with it, shaking our insides like it does so close. It was like being in our own hurricane and it was something to feel. It had gone dark and Mary turned to me. She'd pulled her hood back and her hair was stringy and wild with the rain. She was grinning, her teeth so white it was scary. We were even putting up a bow wave by then.

We started to pass rafts that'd pulled over, the occupants huddled underneath, and she went into her Mighty Mouse thing again, even screaming with the wind. The landlocked boaters waved back, though we must've looked like a river banshee.

We went all the way into Craig like that. She was so worked up I knew there was something alive in there that she was dying to get out. She gets so excited about things. Like this storm. It couldn't have been better if I'd planned it for her. And she's tough, you know. Wind and rain wouldn't touch her. But she has trouble saying things, like tough guys usually do. That's where the whole Mighty Mouse thing came from. She'd get so fired up her tongue wouldn't work and she'd have to flash that grin and wave her arms around like a cartoon character.

We weren't quite so ecstatic tying down the canoe. Rain gear never works all the way and those wet spots were pretty cold once we started moving around. But we stripped it off soon enough and, with the windows fogging up, decided to leave my truck at Wolf Creek so we could drive back to the Falls together. She even sat next to me, like a cowboy's girl, and I put my arm around her, which is not the way we usually drive. I pointed out that with my truck at Wolf Creek we'd be able to float again in the morning without having to drive apart. She said that'd be great and, sopping wet though she was, I think she would've agreed to anything. Her head was pressed into my shoulder and I could feel the water soak into my shirt.

It was still dark when I woke the next morning and Mary's head was still on my shoulder. She was breathing real slow and quiet and it was good just to hold her like that. I knew if we left soon we'd get dawn on the Missouri, and by the reddish light through the window I knew that would be a bad thing to miss. Pretty soon I wanted to get up and get a lunch together and a thermos so all she'd have to do was get dressed— about as close as we get to breakfast in bed. But she sleeps like a cat and

I knew I didn't have a chance of sneaking out. She likes lying in in the morning, half awake, whispering and dozing. She says it's when she does her best thinking. Me too I guess, but if I'm going to have something as rare as an idea I don't want to be in bed when it happens. Lying in bed too long makes my back hurt anyway.

So I tried to sneak out and it didn't work. I brought her a cup of coffee a few minutes later and told her that it was clear out and how the river would be this early with the fog after the rain and how it would smell. She just lay there and said she wanted to stay in and talk this morning since I was here and we could do it.

"Nobody else floats this early," I told her. "We'll have the river to ourselves and it'll be brand new after the storm."

She sniffed at the coffee. "I just wanted to lie here with you and talk. There's things we need to talk about." She touched my hand and added, "You and me, me and you."

I felt the morning slipping away, the fog replaced by fishermen. I bounced on the bed a little and called her a lazy bones or something like that, and told her there were no rules against talking on the river. She glared at me a second then said, "Oh, goddamn it," and threw the covers back and stalked into the bathroom and closed the door. I could hear her getting dressed.

I was pretty surprised and I called through the door that we could stay in bed, it didn't matter. She didn't answer and I stood there, wiggling my toes in my wading boots. When she came out she was dressed and she said, "Let's go."

I said again, "Let's stay," but she gave me a look, took her coffee cup and headed down the back stairs for the truck.

I followed down, not too worried. It was no good seeing her like this, but everybody wakes up like that once in a while. With the river and a little coffee she'd be Mighty Mouse again before I knew it.

It was a stony ride down though, and when she didn't even reach for the thermos I was starting to remember what a nice drive it was last night, with her in another truck. I cracked the thermos myself, driving with my knee, and that smell filled the cab. She reached out her cup and even tried to smile. "Thanks," she said. She never stays mad for long.

She held her cup a long time, looking out over the dawn, saw it reflecting back off Square Butte. The river was nothing but a ribbon of fog in the bottom. Then she sipped her coffee and winced.

"Too hot?" I asked, like there was something I could do about it.

"This is decaf," she said. "It's not what I needed this morning." She looked like her whole world had just caved in.

"Decaf?" I said, sounding pretty slow. I'd only made what was there.

"I can still have one cup of decent coffee in the morning," she said, sounding mean and pissy at once.

"Okay," I said. I poured my own cup. I'd never had decaf and I was wondering what it would taste like. It'd beat conversation this morning.

She drank two cups before we got there, so it couldn't have been too terrible. The only other thing she did was put on another sweatshirt. It wasn't cold, but it would be on the water. I figured she was looking at that web of mist and feeling its chill.

We ran the little shuttle to get a truck at the take-out and then drove to the put-in again—without a word being spoken. The fog was breaking some but the sun wasn't over the hills yet. That would take a few hours. And there wasn't another car or truck at either access. We had it to ourselves.

When the canoe was loaded we stood next to the river a moment. It was quiet, like pin-dropping quiet, but it really wasn't with the water rustling along and a little breeze through the alder and roses. Mist hung head high, so we could see across the steamy river, but the whole world was only as tall as we were, like we could bump our heads on it. It was safe somehow and it had that kind of loneliness that you wouldn't mind having all the time. I put my arm around Mary and forgot to be surprised when she returned the hug.

"Are we off?" I whispered, and she nodded and climbed into her bow seat. I pointed her into the slow current and pushed, the river splashing my boots as I stepped into the canoe.

I gave a few shots with my paddle then gave control over to Mary and picked up the same rod I'd used the day before. I'd set it up this time, so I could at least get a cast in before she asked where breakfast was.

Like I said, I'm no expert fisherman, and that heavy fly was throwing me off and Mary was just sitting there letting the boat drift sideways. I was still getting line out when I saw her hand go up and she said my name and, "Stop." I knew right away I'd caught her, though I'd never done anything like that before. It made me feel sick.

I let the rod down and looped the line out of the water so it wouldn't drag and asked, "Where?"

I was already shuffling along to her seat and saw her holding onto the fly which was in her neck, a little above her collar. The canoe rocked a little, nothing even close to spectacular, and she said, "Go to shore."

"I don't think it's anything," I said. "I can see the barb."

"Go to shore," she said, practically spitting. I sat down where I was and paddled from there.

We crunched into the little pebbles on the opposite bank and I splashed out and pulled us up, saying I was sorry one more time.

She didn't get out and she wouldn't look at me when I crouched beside her. I waited a little, the hook was on the far side, so I couldn't do anything. "Mary," I whispered, and she sat quietly, turned toward the shrouded river. Finally I walked around the canoe and through the tiny riffle to her and squatted again. She lifted her face for me to see the hook and I couldn't have been more shocked if Mighty Mouse had gotten a bite of that blue cheese from the moon and crashed into the center of the Missouri. Tears were coursing down her cheeks, big, rolling drops, one after the other. I stared at them for a second. I'd never seen them there. Then I reached forward to hug her and ask her what in the world was wrong. It wasn't the hook—you could gaff Mary without her giving you the satisfaction of a single flinch.

She leaned into the hug, not sniffing or shuddering—nothing but those tears. Pretty soon she sighed. "Take out the hook."

I let her go some and asked her what was wrong. She shook her head and wiped at the tears, and I knew I'd never get it from her now. I looked at the hook and would have laughed any other time. The point was just pressed in. It was surprising it'd stayed in all this time. I moved it backwards and it fell out. "There," I said, as if I'd solved all our worldly problems.

I sat in the water, next to her in the boat, wishing she'd just out and tell me about it. I knew I might as well wait for rainbows to start leaping into the boat, and when she said I should probably try a fly I knew how to cast I moved back and pushed us out into the river.

She didn't even reach for her paddle, and I knew the fishing was done anyway. So I paddled slowly, trying to make no sound, and I watched the little whirlpools flank my paddle blade as it moved through the clear water. We glided with the main flow, wisps of fog giving way before us and closing back in behind us.

"It seemed like it must be when you're still in your womb, back there," she started saying all at once. "Closed in by water, everything quiet, and everything before you hidden by fog. Everything you might be. Every, every, everything."

She hadn't turned around or moved a muscle. Then she shivered and held herself a little closer as I stared at her back. "What?" I whispered. It was the only thing I could think to say and I was ashamed for sounding so slow.

She shook her head and a little snort of wind pushed the bow to the side and I swept the paddle to keep us on course. Neither one of us said anything for a long time, though I watched her sitting alone, going down the river before me.

The sun finally reached over the hills and touched us on that long straight-away. It's the first place that gets the sun and that we were there was just luck. The last of the mist was gone in seconds, and watching it go I thought this is the prettiest place in the world right now and then Mary said she loved me.

That's not so rare that it'd knock me out of the boat, but it wasn't what I was expecting right then. To tell the truth, I was looking then at the sun and the long hills, yellowed for an instant, and the shine off the cliffs before us. It was one of those times you're afraid will be too fast to see it all, and I'd sort of forgotten Mary was there. Not forgotten, but you know what I mean. It surprised me is all, and I practically said, "What?" again. For crying out loud.

I felt lost in a way. It wasn't one of those times you just say, "Oh yeah, me too, Mar'." It was a bad time for her on a day that couldn't have been better if you'd made it yourself, and she was reaching out for something, to me. And through it all I tried to watch the sun coming up and how it changed everything around me, clearing the fog and giving that clear, soft light to old, almost worn out things, and I felt guilty about trying to shut out everything else long enough to watch.

I was trying to figure a way to ask the question that would unlock what was inside her when the fish started to rise. It was more like the river was rising. First a few, small, slurping swirls, then everywhere, shore to shore. Mary asked what was happening and I thought that's what I should have asked. But I only answered, "They're feeding."

"Catch them," she said, simply enough.

I saw the tiny, black, white-winged bugs and I knew they were tricos—don't ask me how—it's just one of maybe two bugs I do know. That and caddis, which all look like tent-wings to me.

I picked up my dry rod and looked in my box and had a whole row of tricos, eighteens and twenties. That might happen to you all the time, but usually when I do know what's happening I don't have anything to match it.

I tied on the smallest and looked at the river. There seemed no point in casting anywhere in particular. Like flock shooting a thick covey, it seemed you couldn't miss. But I do know how well that works, so I picked a rise and dropped the fly a ways in front of it and let it drift. It went right over and on so I left it to float. It was almost scary, like you didn't know what was under there or what had started them going like that, how they all knew to go at once. So I left the little fly to float, too lost to pick it up and try again for I wouldn't know what to do with it the next time either.

"Uh oh," she said, and I started to look at her, when, out of the corner of my eye, I saw the fly go. I wasn't quite thinking of it or Mary yet, so when I did hit, the line sailed back in limp curls, with the fly floating at the end of all that slack.

"Try it again," she whispered. She was up front of course, and the way the boat and the fly were, she'd seen the trout coming up. That's why she'd said, "Uh oh," before it even got there.

She was hunched a little and you could tell there was something in this she had to see. I cast again, down the length of the canoe, so it'd be right in front of her. I was flock shooting now, I guess, but you do hit one now and then even doing that.

Sure enough, it'd only touched down when that little sucking swirl took it under and I hit back. The way they were all over, the rises I mean, and all such dainty slurps, I was wondering if we weren't into the whitefish hole of all time. But as soon as I hit, out it came, a big, big rainbow, dancing and shaking, then splashing and running cross river, with me hardly doing anything right because I was still trying to watch it shaking in the first sun, when it wasn't even there anymore.

Mary had her paddle out and was moving the canoe around, doing everything right to help me keep the fish. I don't know how she knew what to do, I wouldn't even have thought of moving the canoe. Big fish don't happen to me very often.

He kept running till I tightened up to what I thought must be too much. Then he broke out again and Mary whooped and I tried to gather slack as he ran back in on me, wondering why he even bothered to stay on.

At each jump, with him all silvery, not really rainbow looking yet because he was too fast for anything but flashes of silver to keep up with, he'd have his way. Not so much that he was making all the right moves, but that I would freeze, so I could see him before he was gone. It never worked of course, but I couldn't stop trying.

Even though I couldn't have done anything else to let him get off, pretty soon he tired down some and the jumps got weaker and the runs more easily turned and then he was beside the boat. I held him up front and Mary watched him finning calmly, head into the current, probably wondering what was going to happen to him next.

"Take him off," she said.

I eased him back and he made one last try, ratcheting out about ten feet and breaking out in a jump that had all that was left in him, and Mary jumped up in the front of the boat, giving the Mighty Mouse cheer to the fish, and I guessed to the sun and the river and maybe the whole world that wasn't us in that boat in that second.

She shook her clenched hands again and again, first over one shoulder then the other. I sat in the bottom where I'd dropped when she bounced up like that and watched her, forgetting all about the trout. But there he was, sitting beside the boat. He was ready to come out.

Mary sat down when I reached over the side and cradled a hand under the trout. She sat backwards, facing me, and I held the trout which was like a pet by then, not even quivering to the touch. The hook of that tiny, drowned fly was like the one in Mary that morning. All I did was pull back on the line and it drifted off his mouth without even a flinch.

Mary said, "Lift it up. Let me see it," and I did. It could've been the biggest trout I'd ever caught. I can never remember and Mary says I'm always saying that.

When I lowered it back to the water Mary said, "No. Kill it."

I looked at the trout, which was all rainbow now that it was still, at the rosy run down the line of its side, and the flares of red, and I did not want to kill it. I looked to Mary, because that's never something she says, even when she does want to eat one.

"Kill it," she said again, not looking at me but at where my hands held the fish in the water.

"But, Mary," I started, knowing I didn't have anything to say after that. Nothing was that fish's fault. All I had to do was rub him a few times and let go, but I wasn't sure if I could do that to Mary and whatever was in her this morning.

I started to lift him out again, holding a little tighter since I knew care was no longer required. I was trying, even then, to see just one of his flashing jumps, the curve of the whip-spring body, but knew it was over and I'd never have the time.

Mary said, "Let him go," very softly and I was afraid to look at her because I did not know who I would find up there. I put the fish back in the water and stroked his sides until I felt him stir. I gave him a push then and he was gone and I smiled looking at where he had escaped.

I heard a tiny sob from the front of the boat, and Mary whispered that she was pregnant and that she was just afraid she was losing everything that had ever happened to her before and that she was sorry but she didn't know what she was doing and that she never knew pregnancy would be like this.

I stared for a moment longer at the trout that was gone and I thought I saw him in mid-leap and thought that I would always be able to. And when I looked up she was smiling and there were two more of her big, rolling tears, and she gave the weakest Mighty Mouser I've ever seen, but I could still see her waving wildly in the slanting sun, some-thing whip-springy in her own way.

I'm not always slow, but I still wasn't sure I'd heard everything she said. Me and thinking are kind of like me and fishing, you know? I don't mean I found my brain on the bottom of the river, but I don't ever get so far into it I'm wondering about the pH or barometric pressure of everything I do or everything that happens to me. Mostly that's it, things happen to me. Like this. I don't go around thinking them up. I can't keep up with things the way they are. I've got to react to what happens, and I'm not the speediest reactor, so it was a moment or two before I stepped up and gave her a Mighty Mouse of my own. It was the only thing I could think to do.

Rabbits

I grew up in Idaho, in the desert, which is not a part most people picture when they think of Idaho. It's either potatoes or Sun Valley, right? The desert part is a place no one would visit, let alone live. But that's the way it always was with Pa. He still lives there.

He called me Duke because he liked the way it sounded. My brothers got stuck with Wyatt and Jesse. My poor sister's whole name is Annie Oakley Semovitch. Pa came over from the old country. After the war. Once he went western there was no holding him back. That's how he did everything. It was embarrassing, and I got out of there quick as I could.

When I think of any of that now—usually when I get his scrawled letters asking for money—about all I think about are the rabbits.

We got them right after Mom left us. We ate them then, every single day for three years. But we didn't get them just to eat. They were Pa's biggest get-rich-quick scheme. He was always finding those kinds of ideas in the ads of Outdoor Life or something. Raising rabbits, raising chinchillas, growing ginseng. They all worked into barely surviving schemes though, instead of getting rich.

Same as usual, once Pa got the rabbits I had to take care of them. I must've been around ten or eleven years old. Pa didn't do anything, but he made me responsible for the rabbits. Feeding them, cleaning the pens, rooting out the dead ones before they made the others sick. They took all my time.

He'd take me out of school whenever we got a big order for them. I'd stay home, cracking their little skulls, thinking of my friends in school. The rooms there always smelled like fresh floor wax and we had to sit quiet, with our hands folded on top of our desks. But my dad would already be counting the money in his head, shouting for me to hurry. Not mad, but just excited to get all the dead rabbits to town and get the check.

It got so I could clean and skin a rabbit in way under a minute. With hardly ever making a hole. He was going to make another fortune out of the skins.

At the peak of the rabbit business we were probably up to around five hundred rabbits. I worked like a dog with them. I figured if I could make this one scheme work I'd have something to say when my friends wanted to know what my dad did. If I could keep him on just one thing it would be a lot better. But even when it seemed the rabbits might work out for us, they were still embarrassing. Who ever heard of a rabbit rancher?

Even with five hundred though, I only named one. I called him Panda. I thought pandas were like real bears, you know. Like grizzlies. I thought it was a tough name, not a namby-pamby one. And that rabbit was tough. A huge, black and white male. I kept him in his own cage and never killed him when Pa said it was time for a pogrom. I always thought that word meant a big rabbit order.

I used to like to let Panda out of his cage. He'd terrorize the lot of them. Pound on anything female and bite at all the males. It was my way to get back at them for all the work they made for me.

Panda loved it though. He'd run himself until he was exhausted. That was the only way I could ever get him back to his cage. He was big and I was kind of afraid of him.

But he was embarrassed too. I could tell that, the way he went at all the others. We were both embarrassed to have to spend all our time in that stinking pen of rabbits.

I don't want you thinking Panda was some kind of pet. He wasn't. Panda was just smarter than the rest. He'd see the pogroms decimate the others and knew he was saved each time. Because he was smarter. But I hated them all. Until we got rid of them.

Well, we didn't get rid of them so much. What happened was they all started dying. We lost a few pretty regular, and I'd throw the carcasses out back in the ditch that ran behind the tool shed. But pretty soon there were five or six a day. Then twenty or thirty. I was in a panic that Pa would find out and I'd catch it then.

Panda was all right. It got so I checked him first thing every morning. I was getting up earlier and earlier too, to clean out the dead ones before Pa found them. But it was getting pretty obvious. The pens were half empty. The coyotes couldn't keep up with me and the ditch filled up and I had to carry the dead ones way past it, up into the timber at the edge of the foothills. Some days I'd have to use a wheelbarrow.

It was a lot harder to hate them when they were nothing but knotted up balls of fur. But I knew I was going to catch it for them dying. And wheelbarrowing them all back to the foothills was hard. Some days I'd be all sweaty and dirty before the school bus even pulled over.

I took a licking when Pa finally noticed. He knew I hated them and he figured I was doing something to kill them. Right when he was about to make it big. Mad as he got though, they didn't stop dying.

Then one day he was done with the rabbit business. Wasn't much of a decision—we only had about thirty left and we didn't know if they were even safe to eat anymore. He told me to kill them all and throw them into the foothills, then rip down the pens.

I was a little less excited than you'd think. I was glad to be done with it, but I knew whatever he came up with next would probably be just as bad. And I felt a little sorry for those last rabbits. They'd survived. Panda was one of them. He didn't harass the others as much anymore. I think he felt sorry for them too. It could be he was just sick though.

But I went into the nearly empty pens and there was that kind of frost on the ground that you leave footprints in. I started whacking the rest of the rabbits and throwing them into the wheelbarrow, until only Panda was left. Like usual, I'd put my shirt over his cage so he couldn't see what was going on, but it had fallen off when I wasn't looking.

I wasn't looking either when Pa came up and leaned over the fence like he always did, watching me work.

I went to Panda's cage and I talked to him a little. I told him I was sorry about his pals, but that I figured he would miss them about as much as I would. It was just an embarrassment gone. Panda wouldn't have to worry about whatever Pa would do next.

I was going to let Panda go, you know. I think I would have even kept him in the cage, except I knew Pa would never go for that.

But when I opened the cage to take him out he leaped and bit me on the hand. I've got a hell of a scar from it still. Right here in the soft part, between my thumb and finger. His teeth went clear through my hand.

I jumped back of course, and I stared at my wound till the blood started to well up. Then I pinched it and stared at Panda. He was all cowered into the back of his cage, even though the door was open. There was nothing left for him to leave for, I guess.

"Kill him too," my pa said. That's the first time I knew he had been watching me, and it startled me. I hated his accent. My friends teased me about it.

I held my hand out, to show what Panda had done, and he came shuffling through the gate and pushed me aside. He walked funny-like, looking slow and old but surprising you all the time with just how fast he was. My feet tangled up and I fell down against the wheelbarrow.

Pa reached into the cage and grabbed Panda. Even though he'd just bitten me, I felt bad for Panda. I knew how hard Pa could grab. He had him clear out of the cage and was reaching down to me for my rabbit knocker, which is what we called the little club I'd made for whacking them.

That's when Panda nailed him. He got him three times, just like the bite he gave me, only rougher, because Pa was holding on to him trying to crush him with his bare hands. But Panda just kept sinking those sharp buckies in anywhere he could.

Finally Pa had to let go and Panda hit the ground bounding. Pa's kick didn't even come close. His second jump took him through the door Pa'd left open and he was off for the foothills.

Pa held his hand, swearing in Serb for a second and then ran in for his gun. By the time he came out though there was nothing to shoot at. That's the way it always was with him too. He whaled on me instead, for letting Panda get away.

I started spending a lot of time in the foothills after that. I saw Panda sometimes for the first year. I brought him carrots when we had any. I suppose a coyote got him finally. He wasn't raised up to live wild. But when he was still around we used to sit up in the hills and watch my pa puttering around the place, doing nothing, waiting for his next scheme to happen.

Ginseng was next I think. As if anything could grow in that desert. But my brothers were taking care of the schemes by then. My father said my sap was ruining me, as it did every boy my age. *Efry boy my aych,* is how he said it. He said I only thought of pounding the girls, like my beloved Panda. He said that right in front of my sister, Annie, and I hit him. I was only fourteen and he took the punch. He laughed at that until he roared.

I took off for good pretty soon after that.

About five, maybe six years later, I started getting the letters, asking for money. He found out where I lived, probably from one of the letters I sent to Annie. I was working then, and I was sending money to the school, for Annie and my brothers.

When I saw that spidery handwriting, with the foreign sounding sentences so much like his accent, I thought of my brothers and me staying up late in our room, talking about killing him. We planned it hundreds of times. And, for a minute, when I found out he knew where I lived, I had that same crushed-down feeling, wondering what he was going to make me do next, and I wished we'd gone ahead with it.

But it wouldn't've been one of us killing him, it would've been me. I was the oldest. It would've been easy. There were guns around. All the time. But I always cancelled the plans. I was never sure why, and I couldn't explain it to my brothers, who would get so frustrated I could see them nearly cry.

But he wasn't worth it, you see? My brothers and Annie and me, we each lit out of there as soon as we figured we were old enough. Not one of us finished high school. I went to butcher school when I was fifteen. The money I sent let them get out a little easier than I did, and they all turned out all right. We all did, so maybe it wasn't such a bad upbringing.

It didn't hurt me. You couldn't tell. Nobody can tell. Except for the scar, which no one would guess what it's from anyway.

Killing him would've been trouble and we didn't need any more of that. It would have been for nothing too, since we all got away anyway. He was just something we had to get through. It didn't hurt us permanent at all.

Some people say I could've been a lot more than a butcher. One of my friends said he bet I could've been a doctor, the way I handle a knife. I don't care much for that talk. I've done all right. I like being a butcher. I make good money. Not like a doctor of course, but I never could have been a doctor. I don't mind pain—other people's I mean. It doesn't bother me like it should. I never once thought what I was doing, clubbing those rabbits. It was just a job. I couldn't have been a doctor.

I like being a butcher. The carcasses come to me clean and ready now. I don't have to whack them anymore. They aren't even animals. They're a collection of cuts I have to decipher.

That's why I can't hate my pa. I don't like him, but I can't quite hate him. The war was pretty bad for him I guess. A hell of a lot worse than my growing up. They made him fight on the wrong side. It gave him a collection of cuts he never could decipher. I'm not saying I did such a crackup job. But I can't hate my dad for scarring up worse than I did. I don't know what he went through.

So I keep making the cuts and sending the checks, whenever I get those wheedling little letters of his. It sure beats having the old boy show up at my door wanting to move in, doesn't it?

But I really wouldn't mind seeing him, for just one thing. I'd like to see his hand. It used to be big and hard and dark. But he's old by now and I doubt it's like that anymore, though hands seem to change less than most on a person.

What I'd like to see, though, is the scars. From Panda. I'd like to see how his turned out.

I still look at mine sometimes, when I think of all that—which isn't often, not all that often anyway. You know, it's such a clean cut it's hard to believe. And though that was so long ago, and I really can't remember how it felt, I think about how much it must've hurt and about how quick and sharp the teeth must have been.

Bean Time

She falls asleep as if the whole round world was under her cheek. It's only my shoulder though, the hollow between the bony knob and the thin, hard collar bone. Not much of a pillow, but if I don't lie on my back she'll nudge me over until she can nestle her head in like that. It's not two minutes until her breathing slows and gets a little louder. It's always been like that. It's the same every night.

Once, when we were younger, an acorn dropped out of an oak and chunked her right on the top of the head. We laughed and I said, "Right on the bean!" I think it was a word I heard my mom use, like noggin. So when she wants to put her head down there on my shoulder she says she's ready for Bean Time.

That's when I have my time alone. Seems it's the only time anymore. It's hardly alone, of course. Kerry's breathing like that and I can feel it on my chest, which is naked, because she hates to have the blanket over her face. And one of her legs is thrown over one of mine. But it's alone all the same.

I don't know why I keep my eyes open. It's as dark as a cave in there. The kids haven't needed our door open or night lights for a few years now. But I stare up at the room as if I could really see things. And I wind up seeing them of course.

When the affair first started I was glad to be able to see these night things. It was like taking a perilous adventure, like I saw in the movies when I was a kid—exotic birds calling out as I hack my way through lush jungle vegetation to find the hidden treasures. For a while there I thought I was holding all the treasure, even pouring it through my fingers in wonder. But now, as I try to fight my way back, it seems to be an incredible maze of tangled, choking greenery. The time with the treasure trove gets hard to recall.

Sometimes I even sweat lying there with Kerry in the bean position, so confused is the jungle. She says she loves me every night, just before she drops off. And if I have to shift my position at all and wake her momentarily, she says it again. She says it more than ever before. Thinking of the jungle and the treasure I was so sure I had, I wonder if she's saying it to convince me or to convince herself.

When the affair started it wasn't like the planning for the treasure hunts I saw in the movies, with the dusty natives carrying boxes into high-masted ships that sail the adventurers into the heart of the dark continent. It was as unplanned as possible. She was a client at the office and Kerry was at her parents that week and I never thought anything like that would ever happen. When it kept going after Kerry came home was when I thought I could sift all those flashing coins between my fingers. With the sifting, bean time became the only time I had to myself, like I already said.

Now the treasure hunt has draggled down to the disentanglement stage, same as any time back before I met Kerry. I should have known that would follow, but it was such a long time since then. I forgot about everything except the newness. That's when the night pictures were exciting to see. Now it's the bickering I see in the night pictures, and the wishing I was someplace else, someplace with my family, even when I see her in person. I look extra hard to see what I could have been attracted to. I can only catch glimpses of it. I know I have to slash through the last vines and creepers and break back out onto the coast where the waves gentle onto the sand. But when Kerry keeps saying she loves me, I wonder if the ship will still be anchored out there beyond the reefs, waiting for the great explorer.

I worry about what it would do to her if she found out. It's not worry though, it's more like panic. In those night pictures the monkeys' chattering rises to a scream in the gloomy forest canopy and dark, dangerous faces flit through the broad green leaves that surround me. It's how the greedy explorer always met his end in those movies.

It's not my end I'm worried about, it's her. I should have thought about that before, I know. But somehow I didn't and that is when the sweat comes and I try to hold her a little tighter as if I could protect her from myself. Sometimes I'm so panicked that I squeeze too tight and she stirs and whispers that she loves me before she drops back off. I close my eyes then, but the night pictures don't go away.

When we go to bed we chat or read and just let parts of the day drain away. It's when we used to have sex, but that has sort of drifted away from us over the years. We talked about that and kidded some, but when we do have it it's still as wonderful as ever. Just not as frequent, so I thought it couldn't be a bad thing. I'd always heard that's how it got as you got older. We'd never imagined it would happen to us, but when we started to skip nights, then weeks, I figured it was inevitable and it didn't seem to bother us. Just sleeping with him was still as comfortable as anything the world had ever produced. I put my head on his shoulder and it's like a sleeping potion. It's always been like that, and he used to kid me about it.

I could tell when he changed, when he started to almost hold his breath waiting for me to fall asleep. I always try to tell him I love him right before then. He's not a great one for talking and he seems so alone. I want to leave him with that to give him a little courage. Like telling one of the children I'll always be there.

At first I was enraged. And crushed too. How couldn't I be? I'd been so worried about him and trying to help. Then I found out and I honestly believe he thinks I don't know. That's what hurts the most, believe it or not. That he could lie beside me and pillow my head as he has for seven years and think that I wouldn't know everything about him. My head in the bean position is like a thermometer in my child's mouth. There are no secrets after that. It hurts to know he can tell so little about me.

I can tell it's almost over now, between the two of them. I think it will end before I come to any decisions. Sometimes I think, let it end and pretend you never knew. Other times I think, kill them both. I can't do either, of course. It has taken little chips out of me, every time my head touches his shoulder and he holds his secrets away from me. But it is not a killing offense, and it is not something to be ignored. It's a lousy, guilty feeling, as if I had done something wrong, and I can't believe he would do that to me. At the same time, when he sweats at night, I know it is from his fear for me and I know he is extricating himself from her because of me. That hardly makes me feel victorious, but it's all the comfort I have.

Even so, all I have done is tell him I love him every chance I get at night, when he does battle with himself. I shut out what he has done with her. I couldn't tell him that if I thought of them. I couldn't give myself to him for the support he needs now. It would cheapen me to the point of blowing away. And sometimes when I tell him I love him, just to get him through this, I don't know if he cheapened everything by what he has done, or if I'm cheapening it myself, by offering my love to get him over another woman.

So I don't think of anything. I lie there and pretend I'm asleep and when he stirs I tell him I love him. It's like a mantra I can repeat, practically in my sleep, and I wonder if it means anything to me anymore. Or to him.

I don't know when I finally fall asleep. The clock is on Kerry's side of the bed and with her head so close to mine I can't see it. I hardly sleep at all anymore, but I fell asleep at her apartment the other day. She was furious. She was undressing, and I dozed off sitting in a chair beside the bed. She slapped me and I jerked upright in the chair, wide awake, staring at her breasts straining at the edge of the black lace of her underwear. She was shouting at me, saying she'd just about had it with my exhausted mood swings. I didn't look at her face. I tied the one shoe I had untied before dozing, and thought of how that barely constraining slip of black lace had once seemed so sensuous.

I said I was very sorry, for everything, and walked out of her bedroom and then out of her apartment. The shades were open and it was the middle of the day, so she couldn't follow me out of the bedroom wearing just her bra. But I don't think she would have anyway. She wasn't yelling or saying anything. We hadn't planned this either, but I think we probably both realized that this was the end of it. The same way we had mistakenly recognized the beginning.

I didn't bother going back to the office. I shuffled to the car and drove home. The kids were still at school and I walked one of their bikes into the garage before going inside. I was alone in the house. I tried not to look around and I made it to the bedroom and untied my shoes, without falling asleep this time.

I crawled beneath the blankets and my head was awake as ever in that bed. I tried to multiply three hundred and sixty-five by the number of years we were married and then add on the odd days before that, and subtract off the times we had been apart, which were pretty few. I was trying to find the exact number of nights she had rested her head on my shoulder like that. But it turned out it was like counting sheep and I dozed off.

It was more than a doze though. When I woke it was dark in the room, as dark as ever, and Kerry was in the bed beside me and her head was in the hollow of my shoulder and one of her legs was over one of mine. I listened to her breathing and I hugged her just because I knew I had finally made it out of the jungle.

I hugged her too hard though and she woke up. I could feel her looking at me in the dark and neither one of us said anything and I knew that she had known all along. In a moment her head settled back to my shoulder, filling out the hollow, and her breathing slowed again, and I could feel it against my chest, and she hadn't said she loved me. I almost cried then, out of relief, because, standing there on the beach, with my clothes in tatters and not a thing in the world to keep me alive, I saw the beautiful, tall masted ship heave to just beyond the reef. I wondered how in the world I would get out to it, but it seemed like nothing after all that jungle.

He ended it today. I came home from work and found him in bed, asleep. He hasn't been sleeping much, and I knew it was over. I fixed the kids dinner and told them Daddy was sick. I let them stay up until the usual time and then put them to bed. I sat out in the living room by myself for a long time, not reading or watching TV or anything. I guess I stared, somewhere, but I don't know at what. I don't think I even thought. I tried to go blank.

When I did go to bed I stood in the dark room listening to him before I got under the covers. I lay stiff for a while, then finally moved over to him and put my head on his shoulder the same as ever, to see what it would feel like. It felt the same and I didn't like that.

With my head on his shoulder I thought of how restless he had been over the last few months. Now he was sleeping the sleep of the just, and that was the most unfair thing I could imagine. He was not just. He had done everything wrong and I had tried to help him and now he could sleep like this great comatose hulk, simply because it had ended somehow. She had probably been the one to end it anyway. My help hadn't done anything. I hadn't done anything, just sat there and taken it. I was back to being unable to understand how he could ever have put me through this.

Then he woke up and he hugged me immediately, like he used to. I lifted my head off his chest and looked at him, but it was hopelessly dark and I was glad I couldn't see his face. I did not feel any of his relief and I did not think it was right that he could.

He hugged me even tighter and I put my head back down on his shoulder, to try to start getting used to it again. For the first time ever, I couldn't tell him I loved him. I was afraid if I spoke at all my voice would fall apart. I had been angry and hurt, but now I was scared. He was back and I did not know if the same person had made the return trip. I no longer even knew who he had returned to. I did not know if I would love the man who could do this to me. I lay beside him with my head on his shoulder and it did feel different then and when he kept hugging me I vowed that I would not let one of my tears touch his chest.

Spring

He was tired and we sat on a side hill, whispering and glassing. The sun, low as it was, was warm in the evening quiet, and I looked at the old snow still hanging on in the timbered shadows. Even at that distance I could see the heavy, hard granules that had formed with the thaws and freezings. I lowered my glasses and was in no hurry to leave the rocky, grassy slope we were on.

"I've got blisters on the bottoms of my feet," Harvey said.

"Your boots are too new."

"I'm too old." He looked at me and grinned and I couldn't deny it for him. He was still breathing hard from the long, slow climb up to this spot.

He said he'd killed handfuls of turkeys right here in this little bowl and he pointed out the exact locations of each killing and told me who was with him and when it had been done. I'd never seen a wild turkey and I could not work up any pictures of the hunts, though I looked at the spots he pointed out.

He told me to give another try on my box call and I did and he corrected me quietly. He waited a long time and told me to give one more squawk. He said that was better and that we wouldn't try it again for fifteen or twenty minutes. Then he said that had been one hell of a hard night and he was getting too old for the hunting and drinking both.

I thought of last night in the wall tent with three people I'd only met as friends of my dad's. Harvey had mixed the whiskey with Coke until he ran out of Coke, then he mixed it with water. He called it having a talk with the Lord, because the whiskey was called Lord Calvert. I drank it with the water, and that night, while Harvey cooked the steaks and the stove's heat filled the tent, it seemed like the three older men formed an exclusive club that I had mistakenly been allowed to enter. I felt accepted, regardless of the mistake. I had never hunted with a group and it seemed like I had spent a lot of time less well than I could have.

In the morning though, with the men's heavy whiskey snoring, I remembered why I hunted alone. It was time to be out and my head hurt and my legs did not feel up to walking great distances and these old men would not be ready to go for hours. I unzipped my bag and went out into the frost to pee. I heard a long, far away gobble and I stood still for a long time until I heard it again. It sounded like what I had heard in cartoons, and I could not quite believe it was a real turkey. When I went back into the tent Harvey was sitting on the edge of his cot tying his boots. He looked up and grinned and poked a dry tongue out to wet his lips. He shook his head and said, "Did you hear him?"

I'd hunted by myself all day, following the directions Harvey had pointed out· to me while he stood in the gray dawn with one boot unlaced and his breath smoking out and disappearing. When I had finished the loop he'd suggested, I doubled back, making a bigger one. I called occasionally with the box, not knowing what I was doing, but unable to leave it alone in my pocket. I was deer hunting really. I didn't know the first thing about turkeys.

When I got back to the tent in the late afternoon they were all sleeping. One of the men had taken a long shot at one on the run and had missed. No one else saw anything. They told me where they had walked and I was not surprised they hadn't seen anything. I told them where I had been and at first they didn't believe me. Then they shook their heads. One of them chuckled and said it wasn't a track meet and Harvey volunteered to team up with me for the evening hunt.

I started to glass again, without much hope. I had hunted birds for years—not turkeys, but about every other kind that we have up in these hills and mountains. I didn't believe that you could glass for them. You walked for birds, and when they got up they startled you and you had to make your shot that quickly or not at all. Particularly in woods like the ones in front of us, with the Blues or the Spruce or the Ruffeds.

I saw a hawk coming up the draw towards us. I fixed it with the glasses and followed it until I could tell it was a prairie falcon. It entered its eyrie beneath a rock overhang and its mate flew out. I watched them for several exchanges and told Harvey what I had found. He told me they had been there for years. "Since seventy-three," he said after thinking a moment. Then he told me the names of the people he had been with when he first saw them. My dad was one of them.

I put down my glasses and glanced over at Harvey. He wasn't looking at the falcons, but moving his glasses slowly around the entire bowl below us. His pack was behind his head, and he had planted his feet on a boulder so he could lie back without sliding down the hill. His shotgun was laid across two tussocks of bunch grass, the barrels away from me, the metal and wood held away from the rocky soil.

"There they are," Harvey said. I looked to where his binoculars pointed and saw the other two of our party moving carefully up the creek that formed the bottom of the bowl. There was none of the camouflage you hear you need for turkeys and they weren't hard to pick out.

I watched their careful stalking for a while and could understand what they were seeing and where they expected the turkeys to be. But I could also see in front of them and I knew there were no turkeys there. I started to watch the falcons again. Every once and a while they'd scream and I could hear it after it drifted up the draw and I'd smile.

"How's your dad doing?" Harvey said, using the same hushed tone he had been using since we sat down.

I shrugged but he was still looking through the binoculars. "He's having a bad spell right now, I guess. That's why he couldn't make it. I didn't know until I'd driven up."

I still felt odd being here without him. They had all worked with him, and Harvey still saw him frequently, or so my mother had said when I called her from Broadus, wondering why Dad hadn't met me.

"When was the last time you saw him?"

"I guess it's been about a month. Maybe a little more."

"You're still working in the oil fields?"

"Down by Gillette now. There isn't much left there though."

"Your dad is awful tough," he said, and I didn't say anything else. At his age Harvey probably knew a lot more about cancer than I did.

A little while later Harvey said, "There they are," again, but it sounded like a success this time, not like he was just seeing his friends moving up the draw.

I said, "Where?"

He pointed and I couldn't see. "On the hill on the right. In the second little opening. Six or seven of them. Grazing through the green grass on the left of the opening."

I still couldn't see anything and he lowered his glasses and we went through a lot of that "follow down from the big snag" and "see the rock with the black face? Go up from there . . ." I still couldn't pick them out though and I was starting to be afraid he'd think I was hopeless.

Then there they were. There were seven of them, and they were walking up the hill, picking at the ground and looking around. They were dark against the new grass shoots and there was nothing to scale them against. I'd almost laughed when he said they were grazing but that's exactly what they were doing. They worked the hillside like sheep.

"They're moving at a pretty stiff clip," Harvey said. He was standing already and had his pack on and his shotgun over his arm. "We may be able to head them off before they cross over the top."

We hadn't gone far though, before I was doubting whether we'd get anywhere in time. Harvey was limping from his blisters, and he couldn't keep up a great pace. I was behind him, but it wasn't any problem to hear how hard he was breathing.

We had to push hard at first to crest the ridge. Then we had that to follow around in a long half moon. It'd all be on top of the ridge then and easy walking. And the way they were heading we'd be hidden from them and wouldn't even have to be careful till the very end.

At the top of the ridge though, Harvey sat down on a rock. I was blowing by then myself, but I knew we didn't have time to rest. Even if the turkeys slowed down we didn't have an unlimited amount of light left.

Harvey blew out a long breath and said, "I think the Lord is having a little talk back to me right now." His face was red and he smiled. "And these damn feet." He shook his head and stood up and started along the ridge. "It should be easier from now on though."

I followed again and it was a lot easier. My breathing returned to normal, but I could still hear Harvey's. And the way he was walking— I knew it was a pain small enough he wouldn't want to miss anything for, but it hurt to watch him limp like that.

We'd covered a lot of ground, the ridge finally tipping down some so we were walking downhill and Harvey's breathing grew easier. And quieter. We were about to where we had to be careful. We were at the edge of the trees, after following the curve of the bowl to where it shaded the land so it could grow things besides bunch grasses and prickly pears.

Harvey turned around and told me to go ahead, he had to rest. I told him no, we were almost there. We decided we could rest a second and Harvey talked strategy. We'd hold the back side of the ridge then come across the top when we reached a layered rock pinnacle. Then we'd wait for them to come to us. He told me to go ahead again, that he'd be right behind me. I told him that was the whiskey talking and he laughed, as quietly as he talked. "The Lord," he corrected and turned and walked out the course he had planned.

When we crossed over to the turkeys' side of the ridge we were crouching and being careful about where we put our feet. It was wet though, with snowmelt, and it wasn't hard being quiet. We worked out to the edge of an outcrop and squatted down.

It was too close to talk at all now, no matter how quietly. Harvey waited until we were breathing normally, then motioned for me to use the call. Even his motions were slow and secretive.

I slipped the call out and tried to hand it to Harvey. He wouldn't take it, and he winked after he motioned for me to go ahead. I didn't think it was too smart to let me screw it up now but I went ahead and worked the plunger. Harvey gave me a thumbs up and let me know to hit it again. Then he motioned for silence and started to watch.

We were like that for a long time, watching a small patch of dense, silent forest. Long enough that I could see it getting darker. I watched the lip of the draw behind Harvey and started to think we'd stopped one draw short. Harvey motioned for me to hit the call four times in succession. I'd bugled elk and expected an answer but none came. I watched a tree squirrel for a while then motioned to Harvey that I thought they were one more draw over.

He shook his head and bent to my ear saying they might have turned back down the hill. I whispered they wouldn't do that because of our guys in the bottom. He nodded and shrugged. He put his lips almost against my ear and said if I wanted to cross back over the ridge and into the next draw I could work back to him and I might spook something out, but that it usually didn't work that way. We were almost out of light though.

I nodded and was thinking of crouching up out of my squat when the turkey was just there. I couldn't say anything for an instant. It was huge and too colorful to ever have snuck up on us like that. It stood in the open, materialized, its head and neck a blaze of blue and white. It was watching me.

I whispered to Harvey, "Right behind you." It wasn't twenty-five yards off.

Harvey glanced over his shoulder and blurted, "Jumping Jesus!" and leaped up and so did the turkey and I couldn't lift my gun because of Harvey there in front of me and the turkey was flying as head long as any grouse and Harvey fired and it had no effect.

The turkey's wings were set now and he twisted between the trees, angling down and away, using the hillside's drop rather than his wings to stay off the ground. I couldn't notice the color then, just the size of him and the ease with which he dodged all the obstacles in spite of it. Harvey fired again and the turkey lost a few feathers and was pushed down by the impact until his tail brushed the needles and dirt of the floor. He beat his wings until he had a few feet of altitude then set them again, and I got around Harvey and blew a hole through the branches about a yard behind the turkey just before he glided around the edge of the draw and was gone.

I stood like a fool with my gun half up and Harvey was swearing and laughing and shouting that it was the biggest goddamn tom he had ever seen and had I seen the size of him and how the hell had he missed. He had never seen anything like it and it was just so big it threw him off, he shouted, and wouldn't my dad just about die to see something like that.

I'd been reloading and I turned around then, for no reason really, and coming around the other side of the outcrop that the turkey had used to sneak up on us were three more turkeys, strolling along as if we hadn't just set off three rounds and shouted for ten seconds. Then there were four, then five and I said, "Harvey, are those toms?" They were a lot smaller than the other one, and he was the only one I'd ever seen. In the spring you can't shoot the hens, only the toms.

Harvey whirled around and saw the turkeys and shouted, "Shoot!"

"Are they toms?" I shouted back.

"Shoot!" he screamed again, laughing, and I knew he hadn't reloaded after the big one. "Shoot!" he hollered a third time.

I was following the lead turkey with my gun up, forgetting to aim for the head like they'd told me the night before in the tent. The improbably large body was centered in the groove between my barrels and I pulled the trigger.

The turkeys were moving then, but running not flying. The one I'd hit with the double aught buck rolled away from me shedding clumps of feathers and then was up, running as fast as I've ever seen anything run.

I knocked him sprawling with the second barrel but he came back up and was going again.

I dug in my pocket for more shells and two of the turkeys took off, flying straight up until they were above the trees. I dropped a shell into the right barrel and snapped it shut.

I could only see two turkeys now and they were farther away and in some cover and I didn't know which was the one I had hit. Harvey's gun went off beside me and one of the turkeys dropped down and started flopping out of control like birds do if you hit them in the head.

I hesitated and asked if that was the one I'd hit. I was still shouting, for no reason other than that's how we'd been talking since we gave up the whispering. He said he didn't think so but by then I didn't have a shot at the other one.

I opened my gun and dropped in a second shell and saw Harvey do the same. I walked forward and he was right beside me, hardly limping at all.

We found my turkey before we reached his. It was dead behind a tree, wings and tail spread out as if he was trying to look bigger to scare us away. Harvey went on and picked up his and carried it back and dropped it beside me. I was already cutting out my tag.

Then I heard Harvey start to laugh. I looked up and he was shaking his head and laughing softly, but it was growing, and though I thought he was laughing at the little shake in my hands I started to laugh too, releasing all that had been pent up during the long, expectant wait that hadn't had time to get out in the frantic burst of firing.

He sat down beside me like older people do, holding onto their joints and lowering themselves like a fragile load. He was still laughing and he clapped me on the back and tried to say something, but he couldn't so he clapped me on the back again. Finally he squeezed out, "If your old man could've seen us," but he didn't get any farther than that.

I gutted my turkey while he practically strangled with laughter. I was giggling too, but it was a little strange how he was acting. Finally he was into the end of it, wheezing and sighing and rubbing his ribs and wiping at his eyes.

"Phew. I'm glad he didn't get to see that exhibition." He pulled the turkey into his lap but just left it there, petting the warm feathers without making a move to gut it or cut out his tag.

" 'Jumping Jesus!' " he cried again with the last of his giggles. "Miss the biggest turkey we've ever seen anywhere. Three times! 'Shoot! Shoot!' You jumping around me and me jumping around you. 'Are they toms?' 'Shoot!' Look at the size of these poor little jakes."

"I didn't know the first one was so big," I said. "I'd never seen one before."

"Jack would've. He wanted one like that for years. He would've rather watched us hop around like that though."

Jack was my father. "I never went turkey hunting with him," I said. "I don't know why. We never went out in the spring. In the fall it was always for the covey birds. Or big game."

"Oh, he never went out in the spring. Said it was a shame for anything to die in the spring."

"He was weird about things that way sometimes."

I cleaned the turkey blood from beneath my fingernails with a pine needle and Harvey said, "You know he's not making it to the fall?"

"That's what they say." I lifted the turkey out of my lap and looked at its head. It wasn't as colorful as the big one had been. It was ugly.

"That's why he was going to go this spring. Because he'd never been with you and he knew he wouldn't have another chance."

"He might. Sometimes he bounces back pretty good from the chemo."

"He's not going to."

I looked at Harvey then, because I didn't like talking about this and I didn't like the way he talked about it. He shook his head at me. "He doesn't have two weeks," he said quietly. "He's not coming out of the hospital again."

I stared at Harvey like I'd like to kill him, but it didn't faze him. He shrugged and I said, "Who the hell are you anyway, his fucking doctor?"

"Nope." He looked down at where his hand was smoothing the bird's feathers. "We take each other to our chemo sessions. Your mom can't take seeing him right afterwards. It pretty much knocks you out for a few days."

I didn't say anything and he said, "He asked me to get you a turkey. He would have died if you'd brought the monster turkey of the world in to him."

I thought of Harvey breathing so hard, when we were walking downhill even, and of the way he lowered himself to the ground. "We can get him in the fall," I said, and I turned away when he said no, he doubted that we could.

Then I thought of him yelling like he did when he saw the big turkey and I didn't believe he could really have been that shocked if he had been hunting for all those years. "How come you let the big one go?" I asked.

"I did try to, didn't I?" he said, laughing. "But I couldn't quite do it. I didn't want to kill anything that great. Not in the spring. But at last I didn't want to leave without him. It's that way with everything now. Not knowing what to take and what to leave."

He stood up then, as carefully as he had sat down. "Let's go back down and have a word with the Lord. What do you think?"

I said that would be all right.

I tried to carry his bird for him but he wouldn't let me. "First thing tomorrow we can get back into town and show these runts off to the old man. The three of us'll all have a word with the Lord together."

"I've got to get back to work," I said. I knew it sounded lame, but I couldn't take seeing the old man. I could never think of anything to say when he looked like that. Even if I could my throat wouldn't've worked right for it. Sometimes, looking at him all withered out like that, I thought I'd strangle. "I don't have time," I whispered.

Harvey just said, "You don't know one goddamn thing about time yet," and he started to laugh again.

" 'Jumping Jesus,' " he mumbled. Then, " 'Are they toms?' " He went on a few steps farther and stumbled over a root and went all the way down. I jumped to help him up but he waved me away and lay there chuckling. " 'Shoot! Shoot!' " he said, and he held his shotgun up for me to take.

Eloping

I'd met her in L.A. I was down on a commercial trafficking case, working with the Feds—grizzly claws, bald eagles, velvet antlers, that sort of thing. She was one of the purchasers—no idea it wasn't legal to buy a grizzly rug. She'd had trouble understanding that she wasn't able to buy anything she wanted. But she'd cooperated and we'd netted a good part of the ring, and one thing had led to another between us and now she was riding beside me in Montana, a place she'd never been. We were going to Coeur d'Alene in the next day or two, where there is no wait for a marriage. I guess you could say we were both going places we'd never been.

She touched my leg, asking what I was thinking. I shook my head and she brushed back some of the hair that was hiding her face. It was late in the day, the sun low enough over the mountains that she'd dropped the visor on her side of the cab. But where the sun cut in below the shade, curving across her cheek bones, it shone on her hair— exactly the same color as the dried grasses outside, lit by the same low, gold light. I'd set her flight late just for that light.

I couldn't think of anything to say, so I started to tell her about the rivers we could see, the Three Forks, where the Madison, Gallatin, and Jefferson rivers come together to start the Missouri, and about Lewis and Clark and all that. It was dull though, and I let it die out. It was one of those things you couldn't tell anyway. The sun, flat and silvery on the sloughs, all jumbled and painful sparkles in the riffles said more than the names. I reached over and brushed her thigh, still a little tentatively. But the rivers and the light and the retreating hills, all colored like her hair, gave me the confidence I'd wondered about all the way into Bozeman.

I caught her gaze a moment before she touched the back of my hand with her fingertips and I had to turn my eyes away to look at the highway.

We left the rivers behind, rising into the higher country running up to Helena. She asked about my work, not really caring what I answered, just that I did. As I explained the group of poachers I'd been in with, her mouth curved up at the corners and she closed her eyes against the now annoyingly bright sun.

"Are you at all nervous about giving it up?" she asked in the same dreamy, not quite interested voice. Not uninterested really, but more like she was thinking of something else.

"I don't think so," I said, but then I told the truth. "I don't know. I've always worked."

"We can be out in the mountains as much as you want now. We can do anything you want, and anywhere too."

I saw the way she smiled about my work, and I couldn't help thinking she was making fun of it. But it could have been because it was in a similar operation that we'd met and this whole avalanche had started. I was all nerves by this time, and I wasn't making much sense even to myself.

The "and anywhere" bothered me too. It was like she'd already decided that we were going to leave. That was something we'd agreed to talk about later. Things had happened in such a rush between us maybe she'd already decided to leave Montana before she'd ever seen it and just hadn't had a chance to tell me. It was something I would have wanted to know.

The sun was hard on our left now, almost down, and we were past Helena, on the high plateau just before the road drops to twist through the Wolf Creek Canyon, which is real pretty in its own way. But for just a second the sun was touching only the tips of the grasses, and the ranch set at the foot of the wooded slope was dropping into the shadows. Those long, broad plains, brilliant in the last of the sun, seemed to charge away from the dark timber and up to us.

I turned to see if she saw it too, but she'd already straightened and was gazing out to those plains. She was still watching when the sun dropped and the grass ceased to sparkle and everything went that odd, flat gray of twilight. The sun was still on the trees, rising above and behind the plains, but that was nothing.

"I never expected it to be so barren," she said without turning around.

I'd been watching the back of her head, tawny and alive with the sun on it, while she watched the best this country could give. I'd been trying to calm down and not try to figure what she really meant by every little word, but when the sun winked out she'd seen barrenness. "Open," I said, but it came out as nothing more than a whisper.

She turned and looked at me for an instant and then settled back into her seat. "What?" she asked.

"Open," I said again, too loudly this time. "It's open. It's not barren."

"Mmm," she sighed, making it sound like she agreed. And then she touched me and said, "It's lovely."

But it wasn't, and no touch had ever made me feel as alone as that one did. You had to stay here and work here and go through here again and again before the country let you in, or you had to be somebody she wasn't to see it right off.

"I'm sorry," she said. "It's not barren. I didn't mean it that way. It's everything you are. And everything you are to me."

That may have been true. The land was new and unknown to her, and not excessively attractive. Attraction had been so wild between us that it had brought us to this. But without the attraction there was only the new and the unknown, and the new and unknown were not what they had been. They had never carried fear and regret before.

Glancing over I found her looking at me, as if she were about to ask something. I asked her when she wanted to leave for Coeur d'Alene, just to keep her from saying anything. Coeur d'Alene was the last place I wanted to go at that instant.

She said it didn't matter, and I twisted the truck through the long, swaying curves and we said nothing more. We sank into the gloom of the canyon and she asked again what I was thinking. It was her way to start a conversation, I figured, and it didn't seem too imaginative, but when I looked at her she still held something of the sun and the open in her eyes and in the folded depths of her hair. I thought maybe I could leave this place for her, or with her or whatever.

I reached out and touched her once more, actually holding her as much as I could, to see if that could be true. I had to stop thinking that was for sure. I was in strange country, and I was getting as lost as the hunters from the east do when they first come to the mountains. Struggling against this was as useless and even as fatal as struggling against the quicksand in the Missouri.

I squeezed her so tightly she complained and I loosened my hold, but not much. I told her she shouldn't always ask what I was thinking. I told her sometimes I thought way too much and when I did it wasn't something that would make sense to anybody. It didn't even make sense to me.

She turned to me then, smiling, and making her eyes go theatrically wide. "Just what in the world have you been thinking?"

I laughed then and said it was just too confused.

She toyed with my hand, the one I still had on her shoulder. With the curves of the canyon I had to watch the road but I knew she kept looking at me. "Don't think this is something that I've any experience with either," she said. "My head is leading me on the same wild chases."

She laughed a little, but not to show that she wasn't serious. "I'm as scared as you are about all this."

I did look at her then and she added, "And as excited."

I had to look back at the road then. That or crash into Wolf Creek. I couldn't help smiling though and I said, "I think we should go to Coeur d'Alene in the morning. At first light." The river and the divide, I said, were truly something at first light.

Then she said, "The hell with it, let's drive it straight through."

She hushed me before I could explain how many hours it was from here to there, and what a bizarre route it would be the way we'd been going. She put a finger to my lips and said, "I didn't ask you what you were thinking."

She took my hand in both of hers and said, "Let's both quit thinking. That was always your strong point. That's what you told me in L.A. So quit thinking and drive the damn car, or truck, or whatever it is."

I couldn't help it. I was starting to laugh and I said, "It'll be dark the whole way. You'll miss all the country."

"I'm going to get married," she said, starting to laugh herself, not as quietly as she had before. "You can show me your country after that."

Self Inflicted

Todd crept into the dawn-dark room in his pajamas. It wasn't smoky, but it smelled the way it does after a gun goes off, and like something else besides. He went past his father's desk and, after seeing him, lay beside him on the cord rug. The shotgun lay between them and Todd touched it, his fingers feeling the little scratches that were a grouse etched into the blue metal.

Todd lay beside his father and his gun and imagined the grouse dying suddenly in the air, the way he had seen them do when his father shot them. They flew so fast and so hard you couldn't see their wings, and when your insides were still loose from the rush and clatter of their take-off and you had just barely seen them blurring off, he would fire.

They tumbled brokenly and you could see their wings wrap around them, the tips crossing over their bellies, as if they were suddenly naked. Then they skidded into the bushes.

When you found them they were nothing. Though you could pick them up and hold them, there was no blur or rush left in them anymore. It was almost hard to believe there ever was.

Todd reached over the shotgun and touched his father's trigger finger. He closed his eyes and held onto his father's finger. The shot had woken him and he was still very tired, but he tried hard to remember the blur and rush that was his father. Now there was only the after part, when there was nothing, and he alone, in all the world, knew how he had been before he fired.

The Date

Jonathan sat on the hard naugahyde of the bus seat waiting in vain for his breathing to slow. He wiped his hands against the seat, but it did not remove the sweat. He looked back toward the bus stop, but it was far out of sight now.

She hadn't gotten on the bus. He couldn't ignore that. That might be a bad sign. She'd said she was waiting for another bus. Jonathan had swallowed then and said, "All right," and gotten onto his bus without saying another word or looking back. He wondered if saying she was riding another bus was a polite lie. He wondered if she wouldn't even ride the same bus with him, even though it would mean she would be late for work.

Jonathan wet his thin lips with the tip of his tongue and his hands continued to sweat as he went over it all again. He'd arrived unusually early at his lonely bus stop. He could not now recall why. And then, before he had even settled into the bench, she had flopped down and said hi. He had said something in return, another thing he could not now recall, and it had seemed the bus would not arrive for days. Then she'd started chatting, more to herself it seemed, than to anyone, though he was the only other person there. That was when his hands had begun to sweat.

With all her chatter she had nearly forced him to speak, but he still found it hard to believe he had been so bold, all on the spur of the moment, without the days, or even weeks of agonized planning that always went into the grubby handfuls of seconds it took him to embarrass himself in front of a woman. There was something about her face though, something vulnerable about the way she babbled on so, but would not quite look at him. He had asked her to dinner before he knew what he was saying.

And this woman had looked so surprised, so pleased. She had said yes even as he was ducking his head for the inevitable blow of rejection. He had looked at her then and smiled, smoothly, as if it happened everyday, and Jonathan had no idea where that had come from. He smiled, sitting alone in the bus, remembering that.

But Jonathan's smile faded. The bus had pulled in right then, too early for once. He was standing by then, and he'd stepped aside, to allow her on first, still as if these things came as second nature to him. But she had stepped back and said she had to wait for a different bus. Now, Jonathan was sure he had heard hesitation, and even prevarication, in her words.

Then, as he stood to leave the bus at his office, Jonathan realized with horror that he had asked her to dinner but had been so shocked by her quick acceptance that he had specified no time. The bus had come in too quickly. And her a total stranger. Jonathan stepped out the side door of the bus, so he would not have to tell the driver to have a good day.

When the bus let him off that night, Jonathan gave a quick look around and refused to acknowledge his disappointment. That she would have been sitting at the bus stop at that moment was a ridiculous supposition, one that he had fought down all day. He walked the two blocks to his apartment, angry at himself for allowing the thought to ever happen.

Before lying down in bed that night, Jonathan stood in his pajamas in front of his little mirror. He brushed at the thin, black strands of hair that would not cover his forehead—enough forehead, he thought, to land a 747 on. Jonathan pulled some of his hair down over his forehead but that looked even more ridiculous. He had never tricked himself into believing he was handsome. He brushed his hair back where it belonged.

Jonathan turned off the light. At least he wasn't fat. But he was too tall for his piddling strings of muscle and he lay down on the bed feeling the gangly lengths of his bones. He tried to sleep for a long time before he picked the mystery novel from his bedstand. A few years earlier he'd purchased a light that clipped to the edge of his books. He turned on the little light. The light was sold for reading in bed without disturbing your partner. He'd never had to worry about that, but he liked to be in the dark, with only a light so small no one would know he was there.

He tried to read but he couldn't. He was ashamed he'd been unable to arrange the barest elements of the date. He turned off his little light and closed his book and sat with his eyes open in his dark bedroom.

He smiled though, just remembering the way the woman at the bus stop had smiled as soon as he spoke to her. Her face had opened up as if he were her oldest, dearest friend. If he never did see her again he had at least that. She had almost seemed flattered that he had noticed her. Maybe she really did need another bus.

Instead of taking his Tuesday suit directly from its hanger the next morning, Jonathan looked through his closet and finally chose his pinstripe. He dressed carefully and brushed his black hair, holding it down on his forehead a shade more than usual. He nicked himself shaving but pulled the bit of toilet paper from the wound before he left and when he washed off the blood the cut was barely noticeable.

He stayed back a block from the bus stop, turning the corner at the stop, so he wouldn't be exposed to it for the entire last block. He could picture that; seeing her on the bench, watching him as he walked a block, sweating and trying to walk naturally until he could barely remember which foot went forward next.

When he turned the corner, only feet from the bench, he saw her sitting exactly as she had been the day before. He hesitated, looking at the light fall of her wavy, almost messy light brown hair. It wasn't messy, but the way the younger women were wearing it now. Jonathan had never cared for the style before. He stepped up from behind the bench and said, "Good morning," forcing himself to look at her, not at his glossy black Oxfords.

She smiled like that again, so brightly that Jonathan had to turn away. Yesterday that look had filled him with confidence, now it reminded him of what a botch he'd made of it.

"I hoped you would be here again," she said, and Jonathan knew that was what he would have liked to have said.

He looked back to her and she was still smiling like that, revealing teeth that weren't perfect. Jonathan liked her even better for not trying to hide them. He said, "I'm here everyday. I take the bus to work." It sounded stupid even as he said it.

"That's what I was hoping," she said.

Jonathan heard the roar of the diesel and knew the bus was two blocks away, accelerating out of the turn. He rocked from his heels to the balls of his feet and back, as he did everyday when the bus turned the corner. He saw the bus and read its destination tag, then turned abruptly to the bench.

"I'm sorry," he said, having no idea why he would start by apologizing. "Yesterday I forgot to mention a time. Would Friday evening be all right?"

She smiled and stood up from the bench. "I'd like that," she said. The bus pulled into the curb and air whooshed as the door opened.

Jonathan smiled and nodded to her. As he stepped aside for her, she said, "This isn't my bus." Jonathan nodded again and put a foot on the heavily ribbed black rubber of the step.

"I don't know your name," she said from the curb.

He turned from inside the bus while he flashed his pass to the driver. "Jonathan Howard," he said, and then, after he said good morning to the driver, he turned back to her and said, "And not the other way around." It had been his father's little joke and he was immediately horrified he had said it to her. He had the same name as his father, but his father had been a small, round, jovial man who had always embarrassed Jonathan. It was his father's most embarrassing joke.

The door folded shut in another rush of air and the bus began to roll before Jonathan had even selected a seat. When he realized he hadn't asked her name or where he should pick her up he sat down where he was, without checking to make sure the seat was clean. He wondered if there really were people who could ask another person out to dinner and remember everything and not make idiots out of themselves every time they spoke.

But even as he sighed and pushed his hair up off his forehead he began to smile. She had come back to the bus stop and she had asked him what his name was. And even though he had said that inane joke, which came out so fast it must have something to do with his father's genes, she had smiled at him like that again. He could find out her name tomorrow. And if he forgot to find where she lived so he could pick her up for dinner, he could do that the next day. He almost giggled then, thinking it could be that easy, even for him.

The next day, however, she was not at the bus stop. Jonathan paced back and forth and got on the bus without showing his pass. When he got off the bus that night she was still not there. It was Wednesday night already, and they were supposed to have dinner on Friday and he didn't know her name or where she lived. He hurried home and locked himself inside his house. She would be there tomorrow he decided. She had come back before.

He didn't own many suits that he thought were flattering, and on Thursday he wore the pinstripe suit again. He felt good wearing it and brushing the lapels flat against his chest put down his rising panic. But when he turned the corner and again saw that tousled brown hair he felt he had blundered wearing the same old suit and he wished he could run away.

She turned at the sound of his footsteps and smiled and Jonathan blurted, "May I ask your name?"

"Marjorie. Marjorie Hiller," she said, like it was nothing, and Jonathan barely stopped himself before confessing how panicked he had been she wouldn't be here today and that their date would fall through. But he knew that would be a mistake and he said, "Where shall I pick you up tomorrow?" It came out sounding smooth and unrehearsed and Jonathan smiled at her, wiping his palm discreetly on his lapel.

"I'm new in town," she said, "I don't have a phone yet."

That was not what he had asked and Jonathan thought he caught a trace of secrecy. He went ahead, a little shakily. "Should I pick you up at your home?"

"Why not right here?" she asked. "My home is still a mess. I haven't even started unpacking some of the boxes yet."

"I'll pick you up at the bus stop then," Jonathan said, although he felt a date should not begin in such a mundane location. Then he smiled, thinking that he should know anything about dating.

Jonathan rocked on the balls of his feet and realized the bus had not yet turned the corner. He couldn't even hear it yet. He was sure he knew everything he had to know. Her name was Marjorie Hiller, he would meet her tomorrow evening, at the bus stop, for dinner. He turned to her and asked if seven would be all right. He winced as soon as he added the p.m. What did he think, that he would pick her up for dinner at 7 A.M.? But she just smiled again and said, "That would be great."

Not fine, or just all right, but great. Jonathan rocked back and forth on his feet and waited for the bus.

"What do you do downtown?" she asked.

"I'm a computer programmer for Norco," Jonathan said, embarrassed by the sound of it. He wished he could say he was a detective or a fireman, or even a construction worker. He was a bit relieved to hear the bus turning the corner. It thumped and he knew the back tires had crawled over the curb.

"Computers?" Marjorie asked, and Jonathan turned around at the awe in her voice. "Yes," he said, and he felt warm and important in her eyes, and for once he didn't step aside for her to get on the bus. But he stopped on the steps and said, "I'll see you tomorrow," like it was something he said everyday, and he smiled at her without having to remind himself.

When he sat down on the stiff naugahyde he realized, or thought he did, that she was wearing the same brownish, floral print dress that she had been wearing the other times he saw her. He couldn't swear it was the same dress, even after going through the details of every meeting. What he saw was not her dress, but her face, wrapped round with the shoulder length tousle of hair, and the faded but pretty blue of her eyes. Even as light as her eyes were, the blue stood out under her dark eyebrows. Her hair was too dark for blue eyes. And the freckles that bridged her nose and scattered across her flat cheeks didn't seem to fit either. But the whole, cracked by that open, slightly crooked-toothed smile seemed pretty to Jonathan. Not pretty as in the movies or in the magazines, but pretty to see everyday and not worry about it leaving, or any day turning ugly.

Jonathan hoped it was the same dress he had seen everyday. He liked to think of her wearing a dress to see him, a dress she thought she looked pretty in and that made her comfortable for knowing that. He even liked the tiny stutter that had caught her when she had said her last name. As if she could have possibly forgotten her own last name. Jonathan wondered if it was possible that she was as nervous as he was himself.

When Friday evening came Jonathan had to hold himself from sprinting the blocks from the bus stop to his apartment. He started running his tub before he did anything else. He stood and watched the water swirl in and slowly gain on the sides of the tub. He checked it once for temperature and started to undress.

In his underwear he sat on the side of the tub and touched up the polish on his shoes. He couldn't stain his clothes with the polish that way. When he was done he set the shoes at the foot of his bed and climbed into the tub. There was a crime novel at the head of the tub, but he did not reach for it. He scrubbed intently, using the same anti-dandruff shampoo as always and then worried she'd recognize the smell. He rinsed an extra time.

After drying off and slipping back into his underwear, Jonathan shaved for the second time that day. He smiled when he finished without cutting himself.

The bedroom was cool after the hot, humid air of the bathroom and Jonathan looked through his suits for a long time. He pulled the pinstripe out twice but couldn't wear it again. In the end he settled for navy, which was plain but safe. He dressed in front of the mirror, trying not to notice his high forehead or thin shoulders. He looked much better in clothes and he decided things were going well.

It was only six o'clock though. Jonathan sat in his favorite chair and wondered what they would talk about. Did people talk about books, about silly mysteries? Or about computers? No one ever knew what he was talking about when he tried to talk about what he did for a living, which was seldom enough, he admitted.

He wondered what she did. They knew nothing about each other and for a moment it seemed to Jonathan that that alone would guarantee a night full of conversation. He laughed out loud at the idea. He had never had a night full of conversation in his life. He pictured the silence between them, hot and sticky like the sweat he knew would seep from him with the silence.

Jonathan leapt from his chair and took off his jacket. It was too early to have his jacket on. He paced the room. "I write testing programs," he said out loud, "To ferret out other people's mistakes."

He stopped dead in the room and wiped his forehead with his hand. That sounded too conceited, ferreting out other people's mistakes. And when was the last time anyone said "ferret out" in conversation? Jonathan shook his head and was unable to remember even a solitary shred of any conversation he had heard in his life.

His dad had only talked in jokes, and Jonathan could never think fast that way. His father had embarrassed him his entire life by making fun of him when he could never think of anything to say to strike back. At first his mother had told him not to cry, your daddy's only teasing you. But then she had been sick and she never defended him after that. Maybe he could tell Marjorie about his mother and her illnesses. That would take at least all night.

Jonathan rubbed his forehead again and this time it was covered with sweat. He looked down and found that his shirt was limp already and he hurried into the bedroom to change. This wasn't going to work. He wondered about turning off all the lights and locking the doors and staying home. But she didn't know where he lived. There was no need to take precautions.

Jonathan retied his tie over his clean, dry shirt and started for the bus stop before he could think too long on that alternative. He walked straight and was relieved to see the empty bench at the end of the block. Maybe she wouldn't show.

Jonathan sat down with his feet together and had just begun to perspire when he heard footsteps. Then she called, "Sorry I'm late," and he leapt from the bench as if controlled by wires.

She had a different dress on this evening. It was blue, though much, much paler than Jonathan's suit. It was a match at that, and he smiled at the first success of the night. He looked at his watch and said, "You're not late."

She glanced past him to the street. "Did you drive?"

"I don't own a car," Jonathan said. He pulled a handkerchief from his back pocket and folded it into his palm. When she looked away he wiped at his forehead.

"I know how to drive," he said. "But when my car was stolen two years ago, I never replaced it. I don't travel much." His voice grew softer. "I take the bus to work."

"I'd like a car," she said. "From where I'm from you couldn't make it without a car."

Jonathan stared at her and wondered how long it would take to get a car.

"I've been thinking about buying a car," he said. "But where I thought we might go tonight, if it's all right, is not far from here. We could walk," he said, "Or take the bus."

"Walking's fine. I walk a lot."

Jonathan pointed the way they were to go, with his palm upturned, like he had seen in the movies. He walked on the outside of the sidewalk, to protect her from any splashing from the road, which, with the heat, was bone dry.

He glanced at her now and then, when he could see she was looking at the houses, and then at the shop windows. Her dress was plain sky blue, with white piping around the hem and collar. There were three tiny string belt loops around the waist, but no belt. Jonathan thought it looked nice without a belt, and he marvelled that anyone could have made that decision, just to leave the belt behind when it was meant to be worn.

He also noticed, as he hadn't before, her rather apparent bosom. He thought of the brown dress she'd worn before and thought it had hung straight down from her collar bones to her hips. When he was sure she was looking at a shop window he glanced again at the jutting line of her breasts and he began to perspire gently. The dress nearly hung from there down, as if the rest of her was too small for it. Jonathan missed the other dress.

His mind had been racing for some topic of conversation since he had fallen into step beside her and suddenly he knew it had been there all along. She had said where she came from you needed a car.

"Where are you from?" he asked, knowing this was a good question.

"You wouldn't believe me if I told you," she answered.

Jonathan hesitated. "Yes I would," he said.

"Powder River, Wyoming. Population twelve. Ten now."

"I've never been there," Jonathan said quietly. The mathematics glared at him as from a flawed program. Twelve to ten.

"No one has. I wasn't born there. Gillette." She looked up at him and smiled. "That's in Wyoming too."

Jonathan said, "I've never been there," again, adding, "I've never been in Wyoming."

"Tacoma's nice," she said. She looked back to a window and brushed her fingers along the glass.

"I was born here," Jonathan said, but he couldn't think of an interesting thing about it.

"Really? That must be nice, to spend your whole life in one place. I've never even thought of that."

"What brought you here?" Jonathan asked.

"You wouldn't believe me if I told you," she said, smiling again, and Jonathan wondered if he would ever feel like this would get comfortable. "Oh," he answered.

"I'm glad I'm here though," she said, and just like that she took his hand and swung it as they walked, exaggerating the swing, as he had seen young couples do occasionally. He knew it was never going to get comfortable. "Tell me about computers," she said.

He did. While he talked, without interruption, he looked everywhere but at her and where their hands were connected. She had moved her hand inside his, with her wrist just behind his, so their arms moved naturally, but together. She had done it so quickly he wondered how she had gotten it right.

Finally he said, "Well, this is the place," and he pointed to the restaurant. "I'll stop boring you now."

"It's not boring. I've never known anyone who could talk like that."

Jonathan smiled as he stood behind her and waited for the host to show them to their table. He picked up the wine list as soon as she looked comfortable in her chair and ordered the first bottle he noticed. It came to him as quickly as her hand had, and he smiled again. Things were happening just like in the books.

It was a fancy restaurant and they brought the wine for him to taste. He'd been here before, alone, and he knew what to expect. She laughed as soon as the waiter left, saying she'd never seen anything like that, except on TV.

"You should have sent it back," she said.

Jonathan laughed at that. His laugh was a nasal giggle though, and he stopped it nearly before it started. He poured her a glass of wine and he did not spill any. "You're old enough, aren't you?" he said, trying to think of what his father would say.

"I'm twenty-three. And I'd be old enough for anything, even if I wasn't."

They clinked glasses and he said, "To our date," before he could stop it.

She winked and took a sip of the wine and then another. "How old are you, Jonathan?"

"Twenty-nine," he said, but blushed at the years he shaved.

"I would have guessed older," she said and Jonathan blushed deeply enough for her to see, even in the dark restaurant, and she said, "Distinguished like, I mean. You seem smart and mature." She spoke in a hurry and Jonathan was glad to see her flustered. He took a drink of his wine and she said, "You seem like you've done a lot of things."

"I really haven't. I've never done this before."

"What?"

"Asked a total stranger to dinner." Jonathan could hardly believe he had actually said that.

"We're not strangers, not anymore."

"That's true."

She cocked her head and looked at him through her wine glass for a moment. Then she lowered the glass and stared at him in a way that made him sweat. "Say," she said and reached across the table and pulled his left hand toward her. She looked at the fingers. "You're not married are you?"

Jonathan looked at the same fingers she did. "Of course not."

"I'd do a lot of things," she said, "But I'd never do that. I'd never take somebody's away from them like that."

"Well, neither would I," Jonathan said. "Who would do a thing like that?" He was amazed at the notion, although it happened in his books all the time.

"Lots of people would. You wouldn't believe me if I told you."

Jonathan caught himself looking at her fingers and the waiter returned to take their order and she made him order first, then ordered the same thing herself, saying, "I'll have what Jonathan's having. Exactly." He liked the way she used his name, as if they went way back.

She picked up her fork then and started to turn it end over end, running her fingers down until they hit the tablecloth and then reversing the fork and starting over. "I've never been in a place this nice," she said. "Not once."

"It's not that special," Jonathan answered, but it was the second success of the night, after the way their clothes matched.

They didn't say anything else and she asked Jonathan to tell her more about computers. He did, this time listening more to what he was saying and actually trying to speak in words that she might understand. He watched her closely and added wine to her glass whenever she seemed to want it.

When the dinner plates were set down she gave off a low whistle and said, "This is a ways from the Super Sonic," and then she laughed and apologized when she saw heads turn. She said again that she'd never been anywhere like this.

Jonathan took a bite every time she did, so she would not be eating alone and so, in case she talked to him, he would not be caught with a full mouth. He was generally a careful chewer, but he ate quickly now, so he would be ready to speak at any time she was.

But she ate quickly herself and she only commented on how delicious the food was. It was a simple seafood pasta, but she said she'd never had anything like it in her life. Three successes in a row, Jonathan thought. He had not taken his handkerchief from his pocket since they had sat down.

As they waited for dessert, which Jonathan had never ordered in a restaurant, he asked what she did, since he had spent the whole night telling her about his work.

"I'm between jobs right now," she said, taking the last of the wine. She winked and said, "That's the right thing to say, isn't it?"

Jonathan nodded. He assumed it was the right thing to say. What else would you say?

"I've never had a real job," she said suddenly. "Not like yours. Not a secretary or anything." She raised her eyebrows and shrugged. "But I've worked."

Jonathan nodded. That had not been the right question. He said yes when the waiter brought round the coffee, though he knew he would never get to sleep after that. It was good to have something to hold on the table and something to look at besides her.

"I want to get a good job though. I really do. I think I'm going to stay here. I'd like to start things over right here."

"What did you do before?" Jonathan asked, not at all sure he should. "In Powder River?"

"Bobby ran the gas station there," she said.

She looked up over her coffee cup then, her blue eyes wide over the thin dusting of freckles, and she set the cup down and looked at the table. "Well, I've put my foot in it now, haven't I?" she said.

Jonathan looked at the steam on his coffee, hanging low on the dark surface before swirling into the air and disappearing. He felt the mathematics of twelve to ten explained.

The waiter put the slices of Black Forest cake in front of them and asked if there was anything else they wanted. Jonathan said, "No, thank you," and Marjorie did not look up from the table.

When she did look up she smiled shyly and shrugged again. She picked one of the grated curls of chocolate and put it in her mouth and Jonathan could tell she was letting it melt there, holding it on the very tip of her tongue, where everything was sweetest. "The gas station was the only thing in Powder River and it had been closed for a long time." She looked up. "For good reason. We lost our shirts."

Jonathan didn't answer. He took a piece of the chocolate as she had but it did not taste sweet.

"That's not what you want to know, though," she said. "You want to know who Bobby is, and you want to know about my fingers without rings." She looked right at him then. "I saw you look."

"I don't do this very much," Jonathan whispered.

"Well you wouldn't believe me if I told you. And none of that is any of your business anyway," she said, though not angrily.

"I've never done this, as a matter of fact." Jonathan took a drink of his coffee and patted his forehead with his handkerchief, even though she was looking at him.

They ate the cake quietly and when she said she did not want more coffee Jonathan put his hand over his cup.

"I was awful young," she said, but the waiter brought the check and she only said, "We both were," before she stood to leave and Jonathan jumped up but she didn't wait for him to help her with her chair. Jonathan was certain the string of successes had broken.

She waited for him to pay and she thanked him for dinner as they walked to the door. When they were on the street again it was nearly dark and she took his hand as she had before, but she did not swing it so freely this time. With no idea where else to go he began to walk back to the bus stop.

She looked toward the ground several feet in front of them when she spoke. "Look," she said, "this isn't your business and I don't mean that in a bad way. But this is how it is.

"I'm not married anymore, I guess. I was though, for five years. To Bobby. We dropped out of high school and got married, but never had any kids. We lost everything in that stupid gas station I never could talk him out of, and we drove out this way. Because he knew some people." She sneered the last line, and Jonathan wondered if that was the way Bobby's voice sounded. It was the way he pictured him. Muscular and dirty, with grease on his clothes, speaking with a sneer to pretty girls.

"I didn't know one of those people he knew was a girl, and I sure didn't know he'd just up and leave with them all. All of them except me."

She kicked at something on the sidewalk and Jonathan guessed her hand must be looking like a prune inside his, as hard as he was sweating.

"You know what?" she said, looking up at him without slowing their walk. The day was gone far enough that the street lights were on, and her eyes glistened too much in the light. "He told me I was a joke. Just a bad joke."

"I know a lot of bad jokes," Jonathan said, thinking of his father, but when he realized what he had said he stopped walking and said, "I'm sorry. I never meant to say that."

But she was laughing faintly and she squeezed his hand a little harder for a second. "That's all right," she said. "I know I'm not a bad joke." She leaned against him for a moment before she started walking again. "That was just Bobby. And he isn't even a bad joke. Even bad jokes are funny sometimes."

He put his arm around her shoulders, the same way he had asked her to dinner, without worrying about it first. He did afterwards though, even when she sidestepped to move in under his arm.

"You were the first person to talk to me like I wasn't an idiot, or a bum."

"I just wanted a date," Jonathan said.

"Well you got a lot more than you bargained for, didn't you?" She pulled out from under his arm. "I'm sorry about all this. I hadn't ever figured it would come up. I shouldn't have said anything. I was right. It was only my business."

She had stopped under a streetlight and Jonathan could see her eyes were glistening to the point of brimming over. He took his spare handkerchief and offered it to her.

She refused the handkerchief but said thank you anyway. She brushed at her eyes with the edge of her finger. "You're awful nice," she said.

That didn't leave him anything to say. He asked how long ago Bobby had left.

"Two months. But I know he's not coming back. There are some things you just can't come back from."

They were walking again, but she was a step to his side and she didn't take his hand this time.

They passed under the lights of the little theater that showed the artsy movies that Jonathan sometimes watched and she tugged suddenly at his hand. "Let's go in here," she said. "I'd love to see a movie."

Jonathan tried to see what was playing but they were under the marquee already. "You wouldn't mind taking me to a movie would you? It'll be the last part of our date. I'll leave you alone after that. Promise."

Jonathan did not want her to leave him alone, but he went into the theater with her and bought two tickets. They found seats in the nearly empty room and the show started immediately. "No previews," was the last thing she said to him during the show.

It was a Swedish movie in subtitles and Jonathan tried to watch it but her head was against his shoulder and they were holding hands and he worried about whether he should be changing positions of his hand or stroking her hand or doing anything but just leaving it limp around hers. She did not move her hand so he did not either.

The show lasted nearly two hours and when the credits rolled he was embarrassed to have to wake her up. She had been out hard and when the lights came up she was just rubbing her eyes and she smiled at him sleepily and apologized. "I didn't know it would be all that reading. I don't read that good."

He had never had a woman sleep with her head on his shoulder and he had never watched a woman wake up. He would have liked to hug her then but he waited in the aisle for her then followed her out. She thanked him for the show, even though she had missed almost the whole thing, then she asked him to tell her what it was about.

By the time they reached the bus stop he was nearly finished with the show. She took his hand and they sat on the bench together. "The boy goes to America, in the end. Leaving everything else behind. He thinks he'll get rich, I think."

"Maybe he just wants to leave everything else behind though. Instead of just going to get rich."

"Maybe," Jonathan said. It was late now, and he wondered what they would do next.

They sat without saying anything and Jonathan listened to the crickets. "Are there crickets in Wyoming?" he asked.

Marjorie patted his hand. "I should let you get home." She stood up slowly, still holding his hand. "I've had a wonderful time. A wonderful date, I mean." She smiled at him again and in the streetlights her teeth looked perfect.

"I'll walk you home," Jonathan said. He had wondered since the movie if he should try to kiss her goodnight, and he knew he should try after he walked her home. All night she had been holding his hand like it was the easiest thing in the world and he almost hoped she would kiss him, rather than making him do it by himself.

"Do you live in a house or an apartment?" she asked.

"A little apartment."

"We lived in a trailer in Powder River. One of the old silver kinds."

"Where do you live now?"

"Do you know that first day I saw you? When you asked me to dinner?"

"Of course."

"I wasn't waiting for any bus at all. I was in my best dress, because I was going to a job interview. I just sat down to kill some time. My best dress! That's my only dress."

Jonathan waited for her to go on. He did not want to ask how it had gone if she had not been given the job.

"I had to sneak into a truck stop to take a shower. I dressed up to ask for a job at a laundromat. Can you believe that?" She had turned away from him and was looking up at the streetlight.

"You looked nice," Jonathan said.

She reached behind her and touched his hand as if somehow she knew exactly where it would be. "You're sweet."

She was still looking up at the light when she said, "I got the job."

"I knew you would," Jonathan said.

"I just load the regular washes. But she's already showing me how the dry cleaning works."

"You'll be good at it."

She turned to him then. "A chimp would be good at it."

She pulled a key out of her pocket. "Would you like to walk me home, really? After what a crummy date I've been?"

"Of course. I mean, you haven't been a crummy date." He was trying to find a way to say he liked her, when she said, "Well, you won't believe this even if I tell you." She waited a moment before she said, "I live in the laundromat. Betty, the lady I work for, brought in a cot and lets me stay there."

Jonathan didn't say anything and she tried to laugh. "She doesn't charge me anything for sleeping there. So I can afford it."

"You can stay with me," Jonathan said, the words slipping out from between his lips before he had thought them.

She leant against him for a moment. "I can't do that." She tapped him on his chest with a small, bunched up fist. "I never depended on Bobby to take care of me," she said. "I wasn't ever one of those helpless ones.

"But you wind up depending on something I guess. No matter how much you think you don't. I'd always depended on having a place to stay, without ever thinking of it. Without ever knowing it I'd depended on Bobby not pulling out on me like that. Things can take you awful hard by surprise."

Jonathan wondered what other people did when things like this happened to them—people like the ones that could ask a person to dinner without forgetting to ask what day they would like to go, or even what their name was. "You can stay at my house," he said again. "For nothing."

"The laundromat isn't so bad. It's got air conditioning."

"I don't," he admitted.

"It isn't the most important thing in the world," she said, and they did not start walking to the laundromat or anywhere else.

"If it wasn't so late, you know what I'd do?" Jonathan said, very slowly putting his arms around her back. She was still tapping her fist against his thin chest.

"What?"

"I'd buy a car."

She laughed for real that time, and Jonathan wished she'd lift her face so he could see it.

"I would," he said. "We could drive up to Seattle and look at the lights."

She unclenched her fist then and she wrapped her arms around his navy blue suit and they stood at the bus stop and hugged each other, right where Jonathan stood every day, rocking back and forth on his heels when the bus turned the corner, likely as not climbing over the curb in its hurry and dropping back down with a thump.

"I could buy one tomorrow," he said. "We could drive up and see the lights tomorrow night." She kept hugging him and he said, "They have better restaurants up there."

"I don't believe that."

"I don't want you to stay at a laundromat," Jonathan said. "You could go with me to pick out the car. First thing tomorrow."

She looked up at him and didn't say anything for a long time. She shook her head at the same time she smiled, and it was just like her face, where nothing seemed to fit together until you saw that it did. "I never asked him to leave," she said, then whispered, "I'm just not ready for that."

Jonathan blushed until he thought his forehead would ignite. "I don't mean that." He spoke so fast she laughed again and she was still looking at him and he was able to see her face when the grin broke it and he laughed too. "I didn't mean anything like that at all. I was still wondering if I could kiss you good night." He was surprised he'd admitted that and he blushed even harder and she laughed but tried to hide it and she put her arm around him and started walking with him toward the laundromat.

They did not have far to go and when they were standing in front of the glass-fronted building he waited for her to unlock the door. "Do you have to sleep behind all this glass?" he asked.

"There's a little room in the back. That's where I sleep."

"I don't think I'll sleep much tonight."

"I don't know if I'll be able to either." She smiled up at him and said, "I've got to get one load of laundry done anyway." She did a little curtsy, puffing out the hem of her dress while she bowed. "This isn't my dress," she said.

"I only have the one, and I couldn't wear it to see you four times in a row." She was leaning against the door. "This just came in to be cleaned. It was Betty's idea."

Jonathan still didn't say anything and Marjorie added, "It doesn't fit very well, and we couldn't find a belt."

"It looked nice without the belt."

"You are sweet," Marjorie said, and Jonathan said, "Please stay with me."

She didn't answer right away and Jonathan suddenly hoped she would turn him down again. He would have loved to watch her sleep again, like she had in the theater. And, though he had a sudden picture of standing in his bedroom doorway, watching her waking and rubbing her eyes, he knew he wanted to be alone in his house after this night. He wanted to be able to sit alone on his bed in the dark, with only the tiny reading light on. Everything about it would be so different than it had been before.

"I'm tempted," Marjorie said very softly, "I really am." She touched his hand.

Marjorie started to giggle quietly and suddenly she reached into the modest neckline of her dress and pulled out two balled-up socks. "These were Betty's idea too." Without the padding the dress slouched down her front, too big for her thin frame. Jonathan liked it better that way.

"She'd kill me if she knew I just did that. I may kill myself for doing it, when I think it over."

"I like it better that way," Jonathan said.

She laughed a little then. She pushed the door open but let it close without going through it. "I thought you were going to kiss me good night."

Jonathan stepped close to her and asked, "Would that be all right?"

"Of course it would, Jonathan. But I'm not going to do it for you."

He leaned toward her then and barely put his hand around the back of her head, stopping as soon as he could feel the free fall of curls begin to crush. He leaned down, again feeling the too long length of his bones, and he kissed her on the mouth.

She put her hands on his back, keeping him from pulling away and she whispered, "We're going to have to depend on that, Jonathan. On doing things for ourselves, not on other people doing them for us."

She kissed him then, harder than he had kissed her. "We're both going to have to do that," she said, releasing him.

Jonathan straightened slowly and held the door for her after she had opened it. "I know that," he said. Then, "Can I pick you up tomorrow?"

"Sure," she said, again like it was nothing. "If you're sure you don't mind telling your friends you date the girl who lives in the laundromat."

"I'll pick you up in the new car."

"You don't have to buy a car, Jonathan."

"I know that," Jonathan said and he started to move back down the walk to the street. When he reached the street he turned and she was still watching him from the door. "What time shall I pick you up?" he remembered to ask.

Trash Fish

Every spring the station wagons would pull into that year's knot of midwestern cottages and the family members who had already arrived would throng them, their raucous greetings coming over the lawns to where I sat alone. I wouldn't go over there until I saw my uncle's truck, even though he was always late. He drove alone and he had much further to come.

When my uncle did arrive at the reunions I would be there to meet him. He would hand me my fishing rod then trudge up the hill to announce himself to his brothers and sisters. I would stand behind him then, studying the battered cork butt of the rod and its bent ferrules, trying not to hear the uneasy greetings. He said it was my rod, but always, after three or four days, or sooner if he drank and fought with the adults, he would throw it back into the bed of the truck and drive away. All winter I would think of it, buried beneath the snow in his truck, in the unseen mountains of Wyoming.

When he finally broke away from the family we'd head for the farthest visible dock on whatever lake we had that year. He'd start saying the same things as every year, about how you had to get away from the easy, noisy places to get real fishing.

He always baited the hooks, explaining every time that it was the secret to success. He would wrestle the night crawlers from his wooden worm box full of compost and then shield his hooking process from my eyes. He said he couldn't show it to me, but that if I was a true fisherman, someday I would just know it.

And then we would cast out together and as soon as the ripples had spread away and died on the glassy surface of the lake, my uncle would tip his head to me in salute and take a drink from a flat bottle he kept inside his coat. Then he'd close his eyes and smack his lips and say, "Every year on these old docks I wonder that I didn't have a son of my own." Then he'd open his eyes and wink at me then look out to my bobber and say, "Look sharp!" I hadn't been fooled for a few years but I always looked. It was part of it.

The time I'm telling about now, the last time it could've been good, I was eleven years old, almost twelve. My brothers and sisters were much older and gone, and my parents were ancient. I spent most of my time alone, thinking about things. I never told anyone about my thoughts, but as we lay on the dock, propped on our elbows, I whispered, "It's funny, isn't it?"

"What's that?" my uncle said.

"The water looks so still and everything." I hardly knew what I was thinking about. It just kind of popped out.

"No wind. Dead like, isn't it? Almost like it's been covered with oil."

"Uh huh," I agreed. "It's funny that it could be like that on top, but underneath there's everything. Fish . . ."

"Big fish," he corrected, smiling and taking a sip from his bottle.

"Uh huh. And crayfish and frogs and everything."

"All dead outside and lively inside."

"Yeah!"

"Like me turned inside out."

I looked at him and he was just staring off. I watched my bobber. I never did anything when he said things like that.

His bobber dipped. Not much, but with the flat water it was easy to see. It went down again and he was sitting upright, adjusting the rod to a striking position. I saw his hard hands loosen and retighten around the butt as the bobber hopped around. Then it dove out of sight and a moment later my uncle struck back. He yanked the bobber right out of the water with the force of his strike and guffawed. "Oh, I've got a monster on here, son. A real Nessy."

He hauled the little perch in unceremoniously and dumped it into a mesh basket he tied to the dock, and by the time he returned the basket to the water I had one on too, only bigger than his.

It went like that for half an hour or so. That's the way it is with perch, nothing, then everything at once. He'd rebait my hook, secretly, and point his finger at me and dare me to catch another one bigger than his. We raced to catch the little striped fish, laughing and holding our fish against each other's, bragging and kidding, then putting them in the bucket with the others and trying for more.

It always died out though. The bobbers would sit quietly again and the laughing would still to the same silence as the laketop. "They've passed," my uncle would say.

Then he'd start up about big bass and trout and some other fish that lived in the oceans. He'd say that was real fishing, but it made me sort of lonely.

"How come you don't have any kids?" I asked, wishing he was my father, or at least that he'd had a son.

He took a little sip from his bottle.

"I have no wife," he said, tightening his drag after the small perch. Still hoping for bass.

"How come?"

"Because I never married one."

He gave a small laugh with that, so I pressed on. "Why not?"

He looked at me then and I knew it was going to be one of those speeches and I was sorry I said anything. Sometimes, after he was done talking like that, like I wasn't even there, the fishing would be over and he'd go off by himself. Once he even left the whole reunion and I had to spend an entire year going over everything we'd said, wondering what I'd done wrong. But he came back the next year and handed me my fishing rod and everything was the same as ever. My fishing rod had trembled in my hands and I'd had to stick the butt between my legs on the dock so he wouldn't see the tip waver.

Now he looked away from me toward the motionless bobbers and started to talk the way he did when he decided to.

"I did have a girl once. For years." He paused a moment, then said, "That was years ago, in Pinedale, by the mountains.

"She had a room on the second floor in this old place. But we knew a house we wanted for our own and I was seeing the owner about it and then we would get married and everything.

"But you know how things go. You need money. You can't start a family on nothing—on just wanting to. So I was always looking for work, and finding it too. I was never one who was afraid of work. But you know how Pinedale was then. You couldn't stay and eat too. Every one of those jobs took me away." My uncle shifted his fishing rod from one hand to the other. "Seems I spent more time leaving that girl than I did with her."

He paused a moment for breath. I was digging my finger into the rotten wood in the dock piling. I'd never seen him look so sad. But you could tell it kind of surprised him, like he hadn't thought of those things in a long, long time.

"She had this way of standing on that little balcony and smiling and waving and blowing me kisses until I was out of sight. It wasn't serious, but just a fun, kidding kind of thing she did. And I always laughed, then got down to driving wherever I was going. But once you're driving it's all the same, so you get to thinking and you remember her standing there doing that so you'll laugh and not be sad going to some new place where you don't know anyone. And you know what a good thing you've got and you feel sorry for everyone else in the world because they'll never have it. But then, before you can stop it, you think of her turning back into that empty room and doing not one thing but waiting for you to come back. Then you sit there squinting into the sun feeling small and mean and so trapped that you can't even swallow. I even pulled off the road that last time, I was that close to going back and saying the hell with everything, you're coming with me or I'll go with you or whatever, because there isn't any sense to anything if we're spending all our time killing the best thing in the world. And I didn't do it. Did you know that? Even though I saw it, I did not turn around.

"And I saw it that time!" he said, actually striking the dock with his fist. "She was just standing there, sort of slumped out like a balloon that's been around too long, arms hanging, no smile, no blowing kisses, no nothing, like I'd already turned the corner. Then when I was well on the road it suddenly came to me that that must've been how she looked every time I did turn the corner—and it really was the loneliest, saddest look in the world and how many times had I done that to her?"

He stopped then. I sat as still as I could, praying no fish would take the worms we had out. He looked right at me then, but everything was normal in his face. I looked toward the bobbers anyway. He'd been talking to me like I was somebody.

"You know, I always wanted to go to Ireland. Pa talked about it till he died. We were always going to go, after we got married. A kind of honeymoon."

He was gone now. When he started to mix up what he was talking about it was for sure. I slumped against the dock.

"I was going along the high plains in Montana once—about as far from Ireland as you can get, I suppose. But it'd been a hard winter and all that snow had melted so it was wet and green. Green, you know, like the pictures you see of Ireland with the sheep and the stone houses. But even greener. It was as green as the green Pa used to tell about. Remember that? It was Ireland, you know, and I felt odd about that because it really wasn't anything but the worn out, blown plains of Montana.

"But just as I'm thinking this isn't Ireland, off in the distance, perched on top of a green bump of hill, I see three old men, sitting out there in the middle of nowhere, chatting. They seemed to just grow up out of the green, all hunched in their old black coats like Pa used to wear. And all with heads as snowy as Pa's was before he went. I even began to wonder if one of them might not be Pa, come back somehow.

"And I'd tell you if that didn't give me a shiver. It was one of the nicest things just to see it—three old duffs out in their coats enjoying the sun and the green and as I got closer I slowed down some and was thinking of Pa and how he wanted to go to Ireland and how his life never did amount to much over here and how he'd've piled out of the car and stomped over all that green to sit with those codgers.

"And then it happened," he said. His voice changed and I knew he'd remembered something bad. And I knew right off that that was how I would remember this day.

"Those three old guys in the black coats started to move and as one of them spread his arms it was all falling apart and it wasn't Ireland and it wasn't anything but everyday green. Because they weren't men at all. I'd sure thought they were. I'd known it! But that one wasn't spreading his arms. No, it was wings. And he flapped along, hopping at first, like some giant harpy. Bald eagles. Every goddamned one of them. Wasn't coats and snowy hair, was just eagles sitting closer than I'd figured. Not old Irish duffs, just fish-eating, black and white birds. Would've broken Pa's heart."

My uncle cleared his throat and waved his hand before his face and I picked at the dock. I didn't care about Ireland and his stupid old men. I could've been up fighting with my cousins for all he knew. I glimpsed the bobbers which weren't even moving, just dead.

I think he kept on talking for a moment or two, I'm not sure. Because even as I stared at them, the two bobbers became one. Mine disappeared, just ploop, gone, no tapping or anything. A second later and the drag was whistling out and I held the rod tight and stared at my uncle.

He was up faster than I could've guessed. "Keep up the tip," he said, pointing at the end of the rod, and I lifted it. "Now tap that drag down a notch, son. Let's make him pay for that line."

I did that too, and then another notch as he instructed. And soon I was reeling in, only in spurts, because the fish would run, and I'd have to let him have it. I hadn't said a word. I couldn't. This was the first time I'd ever felt real power against a rod. And with my uncle's quiet advice during the runs and his excited jabber about "big bass" and "real fishing," I thought I might do something to ruin it if I tried to talk or smile or do anything except fight that fish.

"Oh, he's tired now, son," my uncle said after the runs had really started to die out. Soon it began to feel as if there was nothing there.

"Feels like he's dead or something," I whispered. My voice cracked my throat was so dry.

"He's not dead, believe me. He's tired and he's thinking. Running hasn't worked, shaking his head hasn't worked. That's all he knows though, so he's resting and trying to figure out something new. He might do it, too."

That got me scared again, even though the reeling was easy and like nothing. I chanced a peek at my uncle and he caught me at it. "Watch it now. I tell you he's just resting. When he sees this dock and this net," he waved the net he held, "all hell's going to break loose down there. Believe me.

"He's getting close now," my uncle said. He was as excited as I was, leaning out and peering into the flat, leaden water. "He hasn't jumped yet, which is strange for a bass this big. But he will, when he sees how close it is for him."

I'd begun to fear he'd slipped the hook and I was towing in a glob of seaweed. But I was afraid of the explosion my uncle warned of and I gripped the rod harder and reeled in a bit more slowly.

"Now when he jumps you just lift that rod up high. He's trying to give you slack, fast and all at once, so he'll have a second to work on that hook without you pulling on it. But if you keep that rod high, and the line tight, his chances won't be good."

I began a little prayer not to lose the fish when my uncle whispered urgently, "I saw him. Just a flash. Any second now."

He dipped the long-handled net into the water and stood poised over it. "Any second," he repeated.

I could hardly stand it. I continued my methodical cranking of the reel, the handle slippery now with my sweat. I saw a dull, yellow-gold shimmer in the water an instant before my uncle lunged with the net.

"Got him!" he shouted.

I had never stopped that stupid cranking of the reel handle. What happened to the last run, and the jumping? I looked to my uncle to see why he had cheated me of that.

He had the net out of the water and stood for a moment or two, his face twisting. I didn't even look at the net as he pulled it in close enough to untangle the fish. His lips worked momentarily before he spoke. He dropped the net and the fish to the dock. "A sucker," he spat.

I remember being surprised then, and not at all ashamed when I saw the size of the fish. It dwarfed every catch of my life. I stepped toward it to marvel, finally noticing the suction cup mouth and simple, staring eyes—not fierce eyes, as I'd imagined a bass having. I stepped toward the fish and felt sorry for its taint, as if I had something to do with it.

As I stooped to touch the great, misshapen fish my uncle stepped on it. I flinched backwards and stared at him.

The fish made a funny, croaking noise out if its round mouth and my uncle wrapped the line once around his fist and jerked. I could see something pull deep inside the fish and then it gave and the hook came out with no worm on it. There was a little blood coming out of my fish's gills.

"These are trash," my uncle panted. "They eat fish eggs."

He wrapped one of his fists around the fish's middle and said, "Can't even stand touching the slimy, stinking things."

The fish did not struggle. I remembered that first furious rush and the breathtaking runs and felt sorry for how tired he must be. Then my uncle swung around, throwing my fish high, in toward land. I watched, and it flopped a little in the air, even though it was so tired, and then crashed into some trees where I couldn't see it anymore.

My uncle rinsed the slime off his hands and began to bait my hook again. I didn't want to fish anymore. He dropped my hook into the water when he was through, then looked at me.

"You should get used to this kind of thing," he said. "The more you want it the worse it tricks you, or, if it doesn't, you trick yourself." His voice grew angrier. "I can see it in you too. We build these things up in our heads and it's never that way really. That lake isn't dead on top. It's not alive on the inside. It's the same all over. Just a lake. All it ever causes, all this building up, is pain."

He was wagging his finger in my face. It was still black from the mold the worms lived in, with shreds of rotting leaves sticking to it. He was right, I could see things in my head and what I saw now was the rot leaking out of his fingertip and poisoning everything on all those docks. And he was right about the pain, only it wasn't because I'd built anything up. I'd blocked things out. I'd blocked out the rot in him that everyone else could see, but now it was leaking out in front of me.

Then the finger was gone, then he was gone. He left the rods like he always did when he abandoned me. This time I left them too. I wandered over the grass, into the trees where my fish was.

I looked and looked, even up in the branches in case he got stuck up there, but I could not find him. I sat down. The brush was so thick in most places I just couldn't find him. I saw him though, in my head.

He was lying in the dirt with some of it stuck to his sides where the slime was getting sticky because he wasn't wet anymore. There was blood coming out of his gills, only a little though, and he was gasping silently, the way fish do out of water. His eyes looked simple still, but puzzled, and he blinked, which I know he couldn't do, because they don't have eyelids, but he did anyway, because he could not figure out what was happening to him or why. He blinked the way people do when they don't understand something. I stayed there until after dark, when my parents found me, but had only just begun to explain things.

Breathing on the Third Stroke

From the pool where he swam during his lunch hour, Stewart could see the jet fighters from the base drop down for their touch-and-gos. They came in low and straight, following the river, then disappeared into the trees for a moment before shooting back into blue sky, noisier than they were before. The fighters glinted in the sun and sometimes, if their bank was right, Stewart could see the helmeted heads in the cockpits.

He would watch the fighters while he stood at the pool's edge. Then he would dive and begin stroking through the unnaturally clear, cool water and he would not be able to see the fighters anymore. The trains, which followed the track alongside the pool's southern edge, were much bigger and he could see them easily while he swam. He could even hear them sometimes, or smell their thick diesel breath.

Stewart always thought of travelling when he swam. As soon as he dove, and his momentum carried him for a few precious yards through the cool silence, Stewart felt the release he imagined travel would bring. And even when he began to swim, watching the bubbles slice away from his hands, it seemed that nothing could be as easy and soothing as travel. But then he had to breathe and he would lift his head and look down the length of the pool and travel would no longer seem effortless.

By the time he swam three lengths the pain would start and he'd have to start breathing every two strokes, instead of three, and nothing seemed easy anymore. Usually the pain did not get bad and was gone by five lengths, when he would settle into the day's stretch. But whenever he thought of travel it was the idea of that first rough spot that kept him from leaving. He had no way of knowing if the pain would lessen after that, and he had long since passed that painful stretch in Great Falls. He was into the grind now, and it did not hurt much. But he did wonder, every time he watched the jets and then dove, if he wasn't meant to have more of that first little bit, where there was momentum and the initial strokes made him feel strong enough to reach anything.

With the sun, the water in the pool was brilliant and very blue, much more so than was possibly real. The sun sparkled in his goggles when he turned his head and in the first two lengths Stewart thought leaving would be nothing. Recently, the smell of chlorine, anywhere he ran across it, made Stewart think of things that were not quite trustworthy.

After swimming, in the showers, Stewart would try to wash away the chlorine. But it seemed to smell even stronger in the shower and he thought of his wife in the clean, quiet hallways of the hospital where she worked.

Not that she was untrustworthy, not in the typical marital sense. But with the cold water drumming over his head and running down his naked body, Stewart thought he knew so little about his wife that he might well be ignorant of another man. He felt that was untrustworthy —that he could discover after three years of marriage that he knew so little about his wife.

Her name was Kathy and she had red hair—red the color of the darkest kind of maple leaves—that she braided and tied the braids around her head for work. For play she left the hair loose and she had skin like cream, that burned too easily in the sun. Somehow, even with that hair and that skin, she had avoided freckles, and Stewart was grateful for that. She had grown up in Chickasha, Oklahoma, but didn't talk like it. Her voice was low, nearly husky, and she had pretty, tapering fingers. She was long and thin, without much in the way of voluptuous curves. In Chickasha, and then in Great Falls, at the Catholic college, she had been something of a basketball star. There were trophies on the mantle at home.

She laughed, when she did, from the toes, and her eyes squinted nearly shut and her mouth opened wide and she was embarrassed about it, although it was one of the things Stewart had first loved about her. For work she wore a uniform that was as white as the water in the pool was clear and bright.

Stewart let the cold water cover him and he wondered if he knew anything else about his wife. When they had first met and started doing things together and then accepted that they were headed for marriage, Stewart had given her the ring with the diamond, and her hair had been long enough that, when she let it out for play, it would brush against his chest when she was on top of him, if she bent forward just a little. The first time that had happened had been beside the Missouri River, in broad daylight. It was the first time too, that it had been light enough to see all that he could feel and Stewart remembered being stunned and a little intimidated by her nakedness, and he had shut his eyes to feel the ends of all those deep red hairs dancing against his chest.

Afterwards they had lain side by side in the tall grass. She had jumped up much too soon and started to dress. "I can't help it," she'd said. "It's this damn peaches and cream. I'll burn the little I've got right off." She had touched her breasts playfully then, waving them at him and then she'd pulled her shirt over her head.

Stewart had smiled and said, "You're the most beautiful thing I've ever seen." And he'd meant it.

But she had tipped her head back and laughed hard. "I'm a carrot-topped, gangly geek," she'd said.

He had been surprised by that, and almost offended, because it was obvious she wasn't simply being modest. She believed that about herself. The most beautiful thing he had ever imagined. Then she'd said, "And I laugh like a mule, but I can't help it."

"I like the way you laugh," he had answered, and that was true too, though it was the first time he had realized it. "I love it." Then he had looked right at her and said, "I love you too. I love everything about you."

That had still been something new to say, and she said the same thing to him. Stewart remembered how the diamond on her finger had caught the light the same way the river had and he turned off the shower and picked up his towel. He was covered with goose bumps. As he drove back to work he realized Kathy's hair was shorter now. It no longer brushed against his chest. He didn't know when she'd cut it.

Kathy was on the day shift that month, and though their hours were identical, Stewart was the first one home after work. He walked around the silent house, looking for clues to find who he might be married to. He was reading the engravings on the flat brass name tags of her trophies when Kathy came in.

He turned quickly to the door and she said, "Hi, honey." Then she stuck out her bottom lip and blew a stream of air up over her face. That didn't push the few loose hairs off her forehead and she wiped them away with the back of her hand. She moved back to the bedroom saying, "Can you believe how hot it is?"

Stewart followed her back. It was the kind of thing they talked about now, the weather, as if they were strangers groping for some way to start at a party.

He sat down beside her on the bed and unzipped the back of her uniform. She kicked off her shoes, heel to toe without untying them. Then she stepped on the toe of her sock and drew her foot out of it, repeating the process on the other foot. She never wore nylons when it was this hot and she said, "I can't believe you haven't changed already."

"I just got in too," Stewart answered. Her back was just less than white, as dark a tan as she ever took. She stood up and let her white uniform dress fall to the floor. She unstrapped the white bra and let it drop on top of her uniform. Then she dropped back onto the bed, on her back, wearing nothing but her panties. "Whew," she said, wiping again at the hair on her forehead. "This, in Chickasha, is what we call a scorcher."

Stewart undid his tie and hung it on the rack in the closet. He took off his shirt and threw it into the laundry basket. Then he hung his pants over a hanger, and pushed his shoes into the closet with his toe. His socks and briefs followed his shirt into the basket. He lay down beside his wife but their bodies did not touch, because of the temperature.

"How long is this going to last?" Kathy said, and though Stewart doubted she really wanted an answer he said, "What?"

"The heat."

Stewart was on his stomach and he reached out and began to tickle his fingers over the length of her torso, from the protrusion of her hip bone, over the rise of her ribs and the smaller rise of her breast to the line of her collar bone and neck. It was quite a way on her body. She hummed the way she did to let him know that felt nice, and Stewart said that he had no idea how long it would last.

She sat up abruptly and said, "I can't stand this. I'm going to jump in the shower, hon'." She stepped out of her panties as she walked toward the bathroom and Stewart watched as she walked. She was only twenty-six and the muscles in her legs and buttocks flexed when she moved. They had undoubtedly been built up from her running and jumping and shooting. Stewart had met her after her last basketball season and, not being a fan, had never seen her play.

Stewart rolled onto his side and listened to the shower's water running over her. She always stood with her front to the water and she was the only person he had ever seen do that. He pictured the water spraying back away from her body and running down it, coiling around the curves and forming clear lines travelling down her legs. Stewart stood up and followed her path to the bathroom.

He slid the door open noiselessly and though her eyes had been closed she turned to him and smiled. He stepped in and stood behind her, wrapping his arms around her where they were pelted by the cool water.

"Didn't you swim today?" she asked. She tilted her head back so it rested alongside his on his shoulder. They were the same height and she hummed again, to let him know how she felt.

"Yes," Stewart said.

"You're a regular water bug," she said. They began to rock together and then more and they stayed in the big shower until even the little bit of hot ran out and the shower turned icily cold.

Kathy turned the water off and stepped a little shakily from the shower. Stewart sat on the tile floor. "That was nice," Kathy said. She shook her hair, which was still fairly long, and bent so it hung down from the top of her head. She wrapped a towel around it and stood straight again. "How are you, Turban-head?" Stewart said from the shower. He had almost said, "Who are you?"

"I'm wonderful. You?"

"What do you like about me?"

Kathy turned away from the shower and began to dry off with a second towel. "Everything," she said.

"What don't you like about me?"

"Nothing."

The questions had become a ritual. He desperately wanted answers, but her responses were rote and he didn't know any way to change that. He thought he would try hard to answer truthfully if she asked the questions, but she never did. Kathy dropped her towel over the bar and walked out of the room.

Now, he knew, the next thing they would discuss was dinner. As hot as it was they would have only salad, and maybe some bread. They might even settle for slices of watermelon. They would eat on the couch, in front of the TV, watching whatever came on next. Their only contact of the day was making love in the shower at six o'clock and even that had not been face to face. And then she had said, "That was nice," before walking to wherever she had walked.

When she poked her head into the bathroom she was wearing a short, filmy summer dress that she said was the only thing that was cool enough to wear. Stewart was still on the floor of the shower and she looked at him oddly. "What do you want to do for dinner?" she asked.

Stewart watched her for a moment. The dress billowing away from her torso and just touching against her upper thighs was a pale green print of stringing, leafy vines. The cut beneath the tiny sleeves extended halfway to the waist. Stewart didn't think she had ever been prettier and he said salad would be fine. She agreed, saying that it was too hot to eat anything else and she disappeared from the door.

Stewart walked to the bedroom and slipped on a pair of shorts without drying off. He sat on the bed, facing their dresser and he suddenly opened one of his wife's drawers and stared at her clothes. He wasn't surprised to find them there, he was simply curious to see what they looked like.

When Stewart came into the kitchen Kathy was pouring dressing on the pair of salads. She smiled and gave him a bowl and said, "Forks're in the drawer," as if he wouldn't know that. He followed her to the couch and gave her a fork and tried not to listen to the answers and questions of "Jeopardy."

After they were done eating they shared a glass of wine and he asked if she'd like to go for a walk. She smiled and brushed the hair on his head and said it was just too hot. He nodded his head under her hand and left the couch.

Stewart walked to the bedroom and lay down on the bed and picked a book from the nightstand. He perched on his elbows over the white and black pages, but he did not read. They were done talking for the night. There was absolutely nothing wrong, this is just what they had come to. He didn't even know how it had happened. He was twenty-six years old too, just like his wife.

Stewart began two-a-day workouts, swimming early with the high school kids from the team as well as by himself over the lunch hour. He had to get up at six, and he left Kathy in bed every morning. After she went back to night shifts she wasn't home before he left in the morning. They only met in the evenings then, and they watched TV together or he read, and she would kiss him goodnight as he went to bed and she went to work.

He swam harder with the high school kids, and the onset of the pain, when he had to breathe every second stroke or burst, dropped from three lengths to five. It was a milestone, and when he told Kathy she smiled and said that was great. She said she ought to start swimming with him too, when her shift changed again, but when it did she did not start swimming.

Instead she pumped up her basketball and began to dribble around their driveway, twisting and ducking and going behind her back and between her legs and shooting from every point of the drive. She was rusty at first, but she polished quickly and it was amazing to Stewart how well she handled the ball for a tall girl. He had spent all his athletic time in pools, since he was six years old, and had never picked up basketball.

She braided her hair for basketball, as if it were work. It would glint coppery when the sun hit it right. The basketball, more and more often, went through the netting with a slick whish without having touched anything else. When she got up early to practice before work Stewart would watch from the window as he rolled his suit into his towel. One morning, instead of getting directly into his car, he leapt from the garage as she drove for the basket and he jumped, arms reaching up to block her shot.

She was in the air already and the way she traded hands on the ball and twisted her long body away from him left Stewart hanging above the ground with nothing to do but listen to the swish of the basketball through the netting. When he landed she was already dribbling back out toward the street and he heard the flat, repetitive slaps of the ball and her breathing which was hard and fast. She hadn't said anything, or done anything to acknowledge he was there other than twisting away from him and sinking the ball. Stewart watched her, muscles flexing as she reached the street, and he stepped back into the garage and into his car before she had a chance to turn around.

He seemed to hurt as soon as he hit the water that morning, and he didn't finish a lap before he started breathing every two strokes. He gave up after five hundred yards, and drove to work early, having to unlock the office himself. He made the coffee and waited for it to brew, picturing how she had turned away and what he had done to make it so easy. It was a noisy coffee machine and the water trickled into the pot like a tiny waterfall.

The next morning, as Stewart dressed, he listened to the dribbling in his driveway, and the interruptions that he knew were her shots. He couldn't hear if she scored or not, not from inside. When he stepped through the kitchen and into the garage he heard a swish immediately, then the hard breathing and the screech of a dragged basketball shoe and then the slapping of the ball.

Stewart opened his car door and dropped in his towel and suit. She was turning now at the end of the driveway and starting her drive for the basket. Stewart realized she had done this every day, beginning her drive when he opened his door, not just the day before when he had tried to block her shot.

She did not look at him but at the basket as she charged. She faded left around an imaginary defender and Stewart bolted from the garage before he knew what he was doing. As he left his feet he remembered how he had analyzed her shot all the previous morning and he was ready for the change of hands.

But she only faked the change of hands then hooked the ball in with her right as she floated across the front of the hoop. They came close to touching as they were both stretched out in the air, and Stewart flailed his arms too late behind her. Then she was dribbling away from him and he went back to his car and drove to the pool. She dodged around the car as he backed out, then pulled up and sank a shot off the board.

Every morning after that Kathy would begin her drive to the basket as soon as Stewart dropped his towel into his car. He failed to touch the ball, or her, for seven consecutive mornings. On the eighth morning he leapt, more at her than anything else. He had dissected every move she made until it was nearly all he thought about at work. Even at the pool he thought more of her moves than of travelling. The way she soared up reminded him of the jets coming out of the trees, putting on the power.

On the eighth morning he was using his size, getting in her way, challenging her with his superior weight. But somehow she began that beguiling twist and she was nearly behind him before he knew it and he saw her arms extend with the ball and he could already picture that feathery touch and he hacked at her lean white arms with his hard tan one. The ball sank to the asphalt without her arms there to guide it and she screamed, "Foul!" as if he had actually tried to injure her. They landed together and she glared at him, and he could not meet her eyes. He hadn't meant to hit her, he had just been so helpless he couldn't stand it. "I'm sorry," he said, very softly.

"Two shots," she hissed and she bounced the ball noisily to a place on the driveway he was sure was regulation distance. She stood motionless for a second, then, with a light pump of her legs, she arced the ball up and Stewart, looking at her legs, heard it swish through the net without touching anything else. He didn't know why he stayed, but after she sank the second shot she dribbled away from him and he got into his car and drove to the pool. He sat in the stands in his business clothes, watching the high school swimmers churn the clean water back and forth. For some reason there were no jets that morning, but a train did go by, slowing to cross the river on its way out of town.

She went back to night shift the next day and she was not there to dribble the basketball in the morning. When he drove home she would be in the driveway, bouncing and shooting, and she would dodge around his car as he put it in the garage. He didn't challenge her anymore but walked straight through the side door and into the kitchen. She just kept at it out there though, and Stewart switched on the stereo and turned it up until it drowned the slap, slap, slap of the ball.

When she didn't come in to eat he fixed his own salad and started to the living room but stopped at the window in the back door and watched his wife out in the driveway. Stewart was breathing hard suddenly, and his sweat smelled of chlorine. He stayed at the window until she was finished and he had to step away from the door to let her in.

Kathy was breathing hard too, and her sweat made dark patches on her shirt. Stewart was still in her way and without speaking she waited for him to move.

"We don't even talk to each other anymore," he said.

Kathy looked at him for a moment. She held her basketball against her stomach and Stewart thought how odd she would look pregnant, with that lump in the middle of her long, willowy body. Then Kathy dropped the ball into the corner and said, "I'm going to jump into the shower. I sweat like a mule."

She loosened her hair as she went and Stewart watched it fall wet and flat down her back as she walked away from him without saying anything more than that. "No," he said, "you laugh like a mule." She didn't turn or do anything but Stewart could see a tiny hitch in her walk, maybe just a second of a different tension in the muscles of her legs and he wondered why he had ever said that. He loved the way she laughed.

The bathroom door didn't slam shut and Stewart heard the water turn on and heard it change pitch when she stepped into it, face first. He kicked her basketball so hard it left a dent in the wall and his fingers trembled as he looked through the phonebook for the name of someone who could fix it.

After she left for work that night, neither one of them speaking, although he said Goodbye after she had shut the door, Stewart turned off all the lights in the house then turned on the flood light over the driveway. It was time for him to be in bed but he groped through the dark house until he found her basketball. He did not dribble it, but held it tightly between his hands as he walked into the garage and then out into the bright light on the driveway. His first shot missed even the backboard.

He didn't stop shooting and dribbling until his elderly neighbor walked out onto his lawn and said, "I figure midnight's late enough for anybody to play basketball." He took the ball from Stewart and took a shot with his crinkly old arms and missed. "Besides," he said, "your wife is so much better at it." When he was walking across his lawn again, he added, "And more fun to watch."

Stewart dropped his morning swims after that night. Instead he waited for Kathy to leave for the night shift before taking her basketball and shooting in the driveway. He always stopped just before midnight and he never had another complaint from his neighbors. When he carried the ball back in he wondered if there was a way Kathy could tell he had been using it, new scuffs or something. He almost wished she could. Every evening, when he came home from work, she would be out in the drive, firing away.

The last day of her night shift, after which she would have four days off, a vacation they had not even mentioned, Stewart overslept a few minutes and they passed each other in their cars as he drove to work. They didn't wave, but her window was down and he saw her smile. At work he thought of her sleeping at home in their bed and of her smile. She often smiled in her sleep, but he no longer thought he knew why.

At noon, when he drove quickly to the pool, the sky was heavy with clouds, the first for a month, and the wind had picked up in fitful gusts, seeming to shift direction with every new burst.

He changed and stood at the end of the pool. There were two fighters today, flying upon each other's wing tips. They didn't dip into the trees that way, but bellied low then arced into a hard, climbing turn, never looking as if there were more than inches between them. The wind made Stewart shiver and he dove.

The water was actually warmer than the air, and Stewart couldn't remember the last time he had felt that. His arms were cooled on every recovery stroke. It made him last longer, and he didn't drop back to breathing every two strokes until he had swum three hundred yards, a personal record.

When the rain started Stewart could smell it before he felt it. Even over the pervasive reek of chlorine, the clean, muddy smell of imminent rain came into his head and he couldn't have been more surprised at that. It carried the change kind of smell rain has in August, as if everything will be new once it is gone. Then Stewart felt the tiny cold pings on his arms and upper back, and when he turned his head for breaths he could catch glimpses of the drops pocking the surface of the pool. He started breathing on the third stroke again.

When Stewart finished his swim he stood again on the edge. The sky was covered in solid gray and there were whitecaps on the pool. For the first time that summer Stewart took a hot shower.

When he drove home from work that night the rain was coming down so hard people turned on their headlights. He left his off and when he turned the corner to his block he could see Kathy out in the driveway, dropping in a fade-away jumper.

With the rain her old high school basketball uniform was like a second skin, a green one so dark it was nearly black, and Stewart could see every part of his wife's hard, thin body and he loved her. Her hair was down for once. Maybe the rain had pulled it out of the braid. All wet, in the gloomy light of the storm, it was the color of blood that had long since clotted.

Stewart parked his car in the street and sat in it a moment, with the wipers on, so he could watch her move. Then he left the protection of his car and in his business clothes he stood at the grassy edge of the drive and kept watching her. She acted as if he wasn't there, as if he could have been on one of those jets that turned and in seconds disappeared into the distance. The ball, each time it slapped down, made circular splashes that were immediately covered by the rain. More drops flew from the ends of her fingers every time she sent the ball toward the basket, but they too disappeared in the driving of the rain.

When Stewart cut in from the side he stole the ball as easily as if she had let him and he hardly knew what to do with it. He dribbled some but that was a mistake and she had it back before it hit the asphalt a third time. His clothes stuck to him, but he felt light on his feet and he chased after her, but she got around him near the street and drove in for an undefended lay-up.

She retrieved the ball under the basket and looked right at him before throwing a hard chest pass. Then she stood, slightly bent, weight on the balls of her feet, the muscles in her thighs visible in three groups, waiting.

Stewart came in and just as she reached to swat away his clumsy dribble, he pulled up and shot. The ball banged once on the back of the rim and once on the front and then went through the net and bounced on the driveway.

Kathy stared at him, still bent, arm out to destroy his dribble. Then she laughed. It came from her toes and she did not stop right away. Stewart started to laugh too, though it brought tears to his eyes. The rain covered that too.

He took one step forward and hugged Kathy, hugged her so tightly that if she wasn't so lean and so hard she might have broken. She hugged back, even harder, and she kept on laughing. "I knew you were practicing," she said. "I could tell." And that made her laugh even harder. "And you're right, I laugh like a mule. I can't help it."

"I love the way you laugh," Stewart said. "I always have."

"I know."

"I've been thinking of leaving here," Stewart said, without planning to. "I've been thinking about leaving you." They were still hugging each other. If anything, her grip tightened. "Every day when I swim, it's practically the only thing I think about."

"I know," she said. "I could tell."

Then she looked straight at him. "You couldn't ever do that though. You'd miss me until you died from it."

He looked back and their hugs finally began to wear away. "I know. I don't know what I was thinking." Their arms fell to their sides. "Lately all I've done is wonder how I could ever block one of your shots."

"You'll never be able to." Kathy smiled then without laughing. "You're no good at basketball."

"I know that too."

They stood in the driveway with their hands at their sides, looking at each other while the basketball rolled into the street, where the rain was beginning to make rivers in the gutters. Kathy said, "I'm exactly as tall as you are." She said it as a child would, proud of herself for something she couldn't help anyway.

Eulogy

"He's never sicced lawyers on us before," Kagan said, opening the long envelope his wife had handed to him. He unfolded the stiffly creased letter and took a sip of his drink. He could feel his wife watching as he read and he lowered his face so she could not see his eyes.

He folded the paper again and took a drink. "He's dead, Beth."

She started to get out of her chair but Kagan waved her back down. "My brothers will be ecstatic."

"Kagan!"

"He was the meanest man alive, Beth. Now he's probably the meanest one dead. I suppose I should call my brothers."

"I'm sure they know."

Kagan shook his head. "I just got a letter saying my father's dead, Beth. A letter. Not a phone call. He's already buried. This," Kagan waved the letter, "is about his will. He put it in his will not to let any of us know of his demise until all the arrangements were taken care of. To the bitter end, Beth, that's how he was."

Kagan looked at his wife for the first time since he opened the letter. "You know what he left us? Me, I should say. Patrick and Tom got nothing. His moldy, old wooden canoe and his fishing rods. I suppose that's my punishment for sending him the annual guilt letters."

"Those were probably the only things he had left that meant anything to him."

"Well, they don't mean anything to me."

Kagan stood abruptly and paced to the end of the room. He turned and held out his empty glass. "Do you want another?"

Beth shook her head. "How are you going to get the canoe?"

"I wouldn't take it if it was delivered."

"It will be the only thing you'll have from him. The only thing the kids will have from their Grandpa."

"They never even met him!"

"I never met him. In eight years. That's pathetic."

"Well, he'd have hated you too."

"Kagan!"

"See? You take it personally too. It's hard not to, isn't it? But don't. He hated everybody."

"Stop it!"

Beth stood up. "Kagan, I read last year's 'guilt' letter. You left it on the computer."

"You had no right."

"You don't hate him, Kagan. You never could, no matter how much you tried. Why is that something you need to hide?"

"He never answered a single one of those letters, Beth. Never. Not one single one."

"But you wrote them."

Beth smiled at him and held out her glass. "Mix another while I pack for you. You can visit Tom when you go through Minneapolis."

Kagan took her glass and stared into it. She turned down the hall for the bedroom. "You had no right to read that letter," he called after her.

Two days of solid driving from Seattle to Eau Claire. One thousand miles a day. The night layover in Glendive, Montana. It was how he had always made the trip home when he was in college, when his mom was alive. And once the year after.

He remembered how his father and brothers used to meet him out front, charging across the lawn as soon as they saw the car pull in. His mother always stood just outside the door and called for them to come inside where it was warm. And, no matter how tired he was, they would always stay up talking late into the night.

He did not plan to stop in Minneapolis. Tom hadn't lived there when he used to make the drive. But he jerked the car onto his exit at the last possible second.

He had just stepped out of the car when Tom rushed out of the house. " 'Bout time. Beth said you'd be in by noon."

Kagan wished she hadn't called. "Not as young as I used to be on the highways," he said.

Tom's family was collecting around them on the lawn. Kagan shook his brother's hand and said, "Dad's dead, Tom."

"I didn't even know he was sick."

Kagan smiled. It was an old joke about their mother, a famous funeral attender. She would go on about a relative they had never heard of before, fretting about how she would get to the funeral. Their father would lower whatever he was reading and say, "So and so? I didn't even know they were sick." He'd said it so often she'd stopped scolding him for it. It always made the boys laugh. But the joke was the only pleasant allusion to their father made that evening.

As he had known they would, Tom and his wife refused to let Kagan leave before morning. Tom's wife had shooed the children away when Tom continued to tease Kagan about coming for the canoe. And, when the talk turned ugly, she left too.

"I think we could have tried harder, Tom."

"You don't know a thing about it, Kagan. You were already off at school. We still had to live with him. So don't give me that tired old line."

Kagan bowed his head and nodded. "I know. But I can't forget how he was before."

"That only makes it that much worse. Can't you see that?"

Kagan shook his head, not because he didn't agree, but out of helplessness. "He snapped when Mom died, Tom. He was out of his head."

"Please, Kagan. Don't guilt me into anything. You hated him just as much as the rest of us, when it was all said and done."

"I know."

*

Kagan snuck out of the guest room long before dawn. He left a note he didn't mean, saying he'd stay longer on the return trip.

When he reached Eau Claire he did not follow the familiar route to his home but drove directly to the lawyer's office. There was more handshaking, and when Kagan asked the lawyer about the canoe he answered apologetically. "The canoe is in my garage. We had to move it out of the house for the new occupants."

There were more surprises like that. The lawyer wasn't allowed to say who owned the house or where the money for it had gone. If Kagan hadn't known his father he would have suspected a swindle. But he had not been taken unawares by the limitless bitterness for years. He kept shaking his head though, as he followed the lawyer to his garage.

They tied the heavy wooden canoe to the racks Kagan had bought in Seattle. The lawyer found the rod-cases and Kagan put them in the trunk without opening them. The lawyer came from the garage one more time with the paddles and a canvas Duluth pack that looked a hundred years old. "These were not specified, but this is all full of fishing and camping paraphernalia. I couldn't see what good one would be without the other. You don't have to take them."

Kagan threw the pack in with the rod cases and took the paddles. "I don't have to take any of it," he said, slamming his door shut.

"Thanks," he said through the open window, wishing the door hadn't closed quite so hard. "Thanks for everything." He put the car in gear and, just before driving away, asked, "Is he buried with Mom, or is that a secret too?"

"He was cremated, Kagan. He didn't say whether I should tell you that or not."

"Oh, for Christsakes. Well, where the hell are the ashes?"

"I'm sorry, Kagan. That I can't tell you."

Kagan's tire's squealed as he shot out of the lawyer's driveway. "You son of a bitch," he shouted, beating his fist against the steering wheel. If his dad was still alive Kagan could just about kill him.

He drove around Eau Claire aimlessly. It was too soon to get back on the road, but he had nothing else to do. He hadn't been here in ten years. He drifted through the town, finally turning away from the street he grew up on. He turned north accidentally, but held the course until Eau Claire was behind him. For the longest time he would not admit where he might be going.

Kagan was surprised to find that the dirt track was still there. His father was even stubborn enough to fight off the trees' relentless siege. He followed the long, slow curve through the hardwoods and stopped at the tiny strip of white sand at the edge of the lake. He surveyed the lake from that strip of sand and then struggled singlehandedly with the canoe the way his father must have done until he died, at sixty-five.

Before pushing off, Kagan dropped the rods into the bottom of the canoe. The cases rolled back and forth on the dark, glossy wood of the ribs. Finally, Kagan struck straight through the tangle of bushes at the edge of the lake and stooped. He came up with the raspberries he'd known would be there, and he picked until he had handfuls of them wrapped in his handkerchief. He dropped the handkerchief into the Duluth pack, which smelled as mildewy as ever, then pushed out into the lake.

"Like riding a bike," he said out loud after putting the canoe through its paces. He laughed, for the first time since leaving Seattle. His father's last bitter trick had backfired. He was going to enjoy this. He pointed the bow straight across the lake and put his back into the paddling. He didn't care if he would have to pay for that later.

When Kagan entered the left hand bay on the far shore he craned his neck, searching. He looped the canoe around for another pass, but still could not find what he was looking for. He paddled, much more slowly now, into shore.

He nudged the bow of his father's canoe against the sand and listened to the waves hiss away along the small stretch of beach. He did not move for a moment, then stepped carefully over the side, taking the Duluth pack with him. He pulled the canoe up and lay beside it, using the pack as a pillow.

Clouds drifted up from the south, reflected against the far end of the lake. Kagan reached above his head and fumbled in the pack. He found the raspberries and set them on his chest. Still gazing into the clouds on the water, he sucked the first one into his mouth. He rolled it on his tongue then bit down, closing his eyes to hold the taste.

With the sun red-black against his eyelids, and the old taste in his mouth, Kagan let the warmth of the sand work through his shirt and the fall breeze eddy across his chest and legs. Over the small, grassy knoll behind him, just before the dark pines took over, was where the abandoned lodge had been. The one he had looked for from out in the bay. Kagan thought of its long, forbidding logs and boarded windows. They had all been very young when his father first showed the lodge to Kagan and his brothers.

Kagan ate another raspberry but it didn't taste as good as the first. He flattened a lump in the sand with his shoulder. Years and years had piled up since he'd last been here. Or since he'd last seen his father.

The lodge was visible from the left bay, about a mile off, but it melted back into the trees if you didn't find the right spot. Thompson's Lodge, home and hideaway for Chicago's gangsters—as boys, that'd been all they'd needed.

When the canoe had eased onto the sand that day, and the tow-headed boys had splashed and struggled until their father pulled the boat ashore, they'd been off to inspect the building. Kagan had found the one window with the faulty boarding. Their father came up the hill with the enormous Duluth pack and smiled at them, all lined up, Tom pointing up the hill, not daring to speak. He knew what they had found. "Maybe we should see if they left any of the loot?" he suggested.

The decision to sleep in the lodge had come later, out of necessity. Rain had spattered across the lake with the dusk and they'd moved through the window following their father's flashlight. He swept the mouse droppings aside with his poncho and guided the spreading of the sleeping bags.

They'd set up near the base of the stairs. The dim, flickering light of the two candles took over for the usual campfire. The dampness of their smoky clothes and the musty, rodent smell of the lodge mingled. Soft scurryings and sharper taps and gnawings encircled them.

After dinner Kagan asked his father if he was done percolating. Their father's smile was lost in the darkness of his shadowed face. His quietness was traditionally broken around the campfire. The stories were "percolated" with his after-dinner pipe and poured out to them once it was dark enough to be scary.

He cleared his throat and said that he couldn't talk without a fire. Kagan and his brothers whined and pleaded until he agreed that candles could count this once.

Kagan's father's eyes roved about the room, settling on the stairs behind his sons. Taking a deep breath, he began, and the story wove its way through the flickering light in the rough bass that Kagan had vainly hoped would come to him when he grew.

The boys followed the echoing voice along the walls of the lodge into the dismal void beyond the candles' reach. Each log's shadow leapt and quavered as the candles guttered.

But it was the stairs the story revolved around. And, when the madman entered the story, living on the second floor with whispered hints of daggers and axes, the stairs pressed down on the boys until they all leaned toward the candles.

His father's quiet, deep voice rumbled on. He sat back and his face became completely hidden in shadow. Soon he had the grizzled, wild man, dripping wet from the storm outside, easing his way toward the stairs. The collapsing, rotten stairway, leading up to the black hole of the lunatic's abode, crushed down upon the boys. Suddenly they knew he was coming down those stairs for them.

Their father made it impossible for them not to hear each footfall of that descent, and the low, unearthly cackle, and the swish of the final blow through the dead, stale air.

Finally they had all glanced back to the stairs at the same time. Their father had been waiting for that moment. A bellowing, insane laugh filled the lodge and the room was turned into something worse than black as the candles were doused. Without a chance to move, Kagan had been knocked sideways, engulfed in impossibly strong, hard arms, the breath squeezed from him in a gasp.

Kagan opened his eyes and squinted against the brightness of the beach. He sat up and brushed the sand from his back. He remembered his father relighting the candles and soothing Tom, the youngest of them. The attack had been in fun, he'd explained. He hadn't meant to scare them that badly. It was just a ghost story.

Kagan started to laugh. He'd have to go home through Minneapolis now, just to thank Tom for crying at that awful moment. It had stopped their father's attack and Kagan, who had been too old to cry, had been saved the embarrassment.

The short laugh died out on the quiet beach. Kagan plunked a stone into the water, breaking apart the reflection of the clouds. He knew the spot from the left bay as well as his father had. The lodge was no longer there. Kagan knew he should go up the hill and find out what had happened, if it had burned, or been moved or whatever.

Kagan ate another raspberry but it was dry and seedy in his mouth. He picked himself up from the beach, not bothering to brush away the sand. He was stiff already from that little bit of paddling, and the trudge up the hill was longer than he remembered.

He came to the great open square in the trees. He could still make out foundation lines and he pictured how tightly the branches must have closed around the lodge. There were still bits of blackened metal about, and sodden lumps of gray ash. Some of the trees bore blackened scars along the lodge side of their trunks. It all looked fairly recent, but he felt certain his father had known.

Kagan kicked at an ash pile and tried to remember that quiet rumbling of his father's voice caught up in a story, but the other came back—the cutting edge of that beautiful bass, sharper than any knife. And Kagan remembered how, starting even before their mother's funeral, he had slashed and slashed until his isolation was inviolate even to Kagan.

He realized, as he had at the time, that it wasn't them that his father had struck at, but at himself. He had cut himself off from everything that reminded him of her. Her children included.

But knowing that hadn't helped. Kagan turned away from the empty hole where the lodge had been and walked back toward the beach. He settled the pack into the canoe and pushed it away from the shore. He looked once more at the grassy slope that just hid the lodge from view, then walked across the clean sand and through the water to the canoe which was now his. The small wave ridges on the bottom held his weight without giving away, stinging his numbed bare feet.

Kagan backed off shore and spun the long canoe toward the fleecy clouds that continued to drift up from the south. The rod cases rolled slightly on the canoe's ribs. He paddled away from shore, keeping his back to the lodge's beach.

Kagan put his paddle down suddenly and picked up one of the cases. Even as he fumbled with the threaded lid, Kagan pictured the glossy layer of yellowy varnish on the bamboo splits, knowing that his father would never have let these slip away from him. And when the rod slid out and he peeled away the felt wrapping, that's exactly how they were.

He found the reel case in the Duluth pack and though his hands were shaking now, he threaded the line through the guides and made his first cast in ten years, short and awkward, and he could see his father smiling at that.

The canoe drifted in the spot where it had once been possible to see the lodge and Kagan made another cast and watched the flyless leader as if something could still come up to it. Now Kagan could see the lodge and he could see his father standing by it. He knew where his ashes were and he knew the canoe and the rods were not one last cruel joke. He gripped the cork butt of the rod more tightly, feeling the rough spot where his father had stuck the flies, and he made one more cast, toward his father and his lodge.

Shooting Stars

The surviving headlight cut a narrow path through the blackness while Sally and the baby slept, and, though it was far from quiet, it seemed as silent as any time Frank had ever known. The radio's muted static blended with the constant hum of motor and road that filled the car like cotton. He shut it off. It was impossible to find anything in the corner of the state here, even at night, and Frank wondered what the Indians lived by. It was a hell of a place for people, even for a reservation.

A moment later Frank turned the radio back on, not far enough for sound, but just for its glow. He hated being alone more than anything in the world. But the tires' hiss and the noise of the wind and the glow of the radio were all the company he cared for now. By morning they would be at Crow Agency and he would need Sally then, when the pale winter light glared on every detail of the desolation surrounding them.

Frank watched the patch of lighted road, curving with it. No guard-rails, no reflectors showing the shoulder, not even a line painted down the middle. How in the world was a person supposed to even see this goddamned road, let alone stay on it? And with only one headlight? Frank wondered what the Indians had done to deserve this piece of nowhere. The only thing to do if you were born here was to leave. But the road made even that harrowing. Dakota, Wyoming, Montana. They would all be bad jokes if they weren't true.

He remembered her reading the road map early the day before, discovering that Custer had been massacred at Crow Agency. He barely remembered the history, but now he felt sorry for Custer. And for the Indians. It was understandable why they'd want to stay here, at the site of their only victory, but it was pathetic. You had to move on. Victories came far enough apart it was best to not even remember them.

The road was ridiculous. It was impossible to miss all the potholes. At each jarring he flinched, fearing the baby would wake. If it cried once more he could just about roll down the window and throw it into the void they were drifting through.

That wasn't true. It was awful to even think of it. Yet, even though he would die before doing something like that, it would be doing something. Something that would mean being in control of his own future for an instant anyway.

The baby was a hell of a mess. He loved it, he guessed. It was a good thing to be a father. There was a feeling to it he hadn't expected. But he thought he'd have liked it just for being. How did other people do it? How did they love something so much that only made everything that much harder?

He almost glanced at them sleeping together against the far door, but the pitch of the constant hum surrounding him changed suddenly. Frank tensed and checked the dashboard. There were no gauges though, nothing to tell him if the old wreck was failing. Only idiot lights. They'd turn red, if they worked at all, long after the trouble turned hopeless. Cars this old didn't take long to disintegrate. Frank was no mechanic, but he knew that.

Frank looked into the mirror but the back seat was loaded floor to ceiling. There were no other cars out here. Frank couldn't remember the last one he had seen. He checked the dashboard one more time and took a deep breath. Maybe it was just a different kind of asphalt or pavement. Maybe the car was eating itself alive. It really didn't make much difference. Who would he have fix it out here? Geronimo? Frank smiled. Geronimo would have to work for nothing. That's how much Frank could afford. What a great time to have a baby.

When Sally had told him she was pregnant, he had said maybe they could sue the pill company and finally get their feet under them. He held her afterwards, apologizing, and never told her he had nearly been serious.

Frank squeezed the steering wheel and shook it. How in the world could work be so impossible to find? And what good was it to spend even the last untouchable bit to go somewhere new? He did look at Sally now, though she was just a lump against the door, with only her hair showing faintly in the reflection of the headlight. Leaving had been his idea, he admitted, but had Des Moines really been as hopeless as this?

The road noises that enveloped Frank and his family changed again. This time Frank could feel it, through the steering wheel and in the cold twisting of his stomach. It was under the hood. Probably had been all along. He rubbed at his face. It felt like warm rubber under his palm and he wondered how late it was. After three for sure. He couldn't read his watch in the dark. The wobbly sound under the hood grew harsher, squealed wildly for a moment, then settled into a rasping throb.

Sally hadn't stirred. He could hardly believe she had slept through that screaming. It had instantly brought sticky, stupid sweat out of him. It sounded almost human. The engine was quieter now but still all wrong. He looked at the dash and cursed the vacant idiot lights. He kept the speedometer on sixty, and waited for the dashboard to flare up. Then he pushed it to sixty-five. Take the old piece of junk to hell anyway.

He edged the car through a curve that he was going too fast for but he refused to slow down. Some of their belongings shifted in the back but the car straightened out again and Frank eased slightly into the slick seat. Then he saw the first spark. It appeared through one of the slots at the edge of the hood and slipped over the windshield like a tracer. It was followed a moment later by a second one. But this was bigger. It was a piece of something. Something red hot, leaving a trail, like a falling star.

Frank eased off the accelerator a touch, and rubbed at his eyes, almost surprised not to find tears there. You were supposed to wish on stars like that. For the next few minutes Frank watched the sparks come from beneath the hood, escaping through the slots. They seemed to be moving very fast by the time they reached that point, then they slowed to swoop over the windshield. He made his wishes when they slowed, then watched them tear off on their missions. There was a cushion of air just in front of the windshield that kept all but the largest chunks from actually striking the glass. Those that did hit made a tiny chinking noise, then swept away like all the others. Frank did not wish on the ones that struck the glass. He turned the static up a little to drown their menacing instants of sound.

He felt foolish wishing and he kept glancing at the dash, waiting for the warning lights to tell him it was over. They did not light up though, and he wondered if perhaps the first wish hadn't had some effect. It was impossible that the car could be tearing itself apart in such a way that even he could see it was fatal but still motor as smoothly as ever.

Frank didn't push harder on the accelerator or change anything else. It wasn't possible but there was nothing else to do. They'd probably die if he had to stop. They'd probably be scalped by all the Indians living off that hundred-year-old massacre.

He heard Sally's sleepy voice and he sprang for the radio volume already knowing it was too late. "How pretty," she said. "Are they fireflies?"

Frank smiled at that. "No. They're shooting stars. There are no fireflies in January. They must fly south with the birds."

She gave the giggle she always did when she knew she was being teased. "They aren't shooting stars, Frank. They're going the wrong way. Shooting stars fall down."

Frank loved her voice, so dreamy with sleep. "They're shooting stars all right," he said. "These are a special kind just for us though. They go straight to heaven so our wishes get answered sooner." It was the kind of thing a father should say.

"What have you been wishing?" she asked.

"I can't tell. You know that. But you better get started yourself. No telling how long these will last. It's been a regular meteor shower."

Sally slid over in her seat, moving the baby as if it were an overfilled jar of something that mustn't be spilled. She rested her head against his shoulder. "What should we wish for?"

Where do you start, Frank wondered. The meteor shower was beginning to wane and he thought, from her angle, she might just think they were falling stars. There were no longer any of the big, ugly ones that struck the windshield. Still the car ran on. "I guess we should wish the Indians don't massacre us."

She giggled again and Frank wanted to put his arm around her. He was afraid to take it off the wheel though. There was no telling what the car might do. Maybe he should get it off the road. What if it blew up? He thought of Sally hurt and was sweating again. "Make some wishes quick, honey. This can't go on much longer."

"I wish you weren't sad."

"I'm not sad, Sal'. But you can't tell me your wish."

"Okay," she said, and then was quiet for a moment. "All right, there."

"There? You're done? Sally, we could really use some wishing."

"Not that much."

Frank glanced at her and there was a thump beneath the hood and they both heard something drop onto the road and clang as it bounced between the car and the pavement. Then there was silence. No lights had come on and the falling stars stopped.

"What was that Frank?" The dreamy kidding was gone from her voice. "Really, this time. What's been going on?" She straightened in her seat, still holding the baby as if she were a shock absorber. Frank missed her touch against his side.

"It's the car," he said, the truth as dull as ever. "Something is burning up inside it."

"Oh," she said. Then, "Pull over, Frank."

Frank was already decelerating. "Maybe we just took a burning arrow," he said.

"Pull over now! How long has this been going on?" She was a mother now, and probably worrying about an explosion. Frank realized he had not even thought of the baby.

"There are no warning lights," he whispered.

"For Christsakes, Frank! Who needs warning lights when pieces of your car are melting before your eyes?"

He didn't answer and the gravel on the frozen shoulder crunched under the tires. They coasted to a stop. Frank didn't want to turn the car off. At least it was still running. He buttoned his coat but with it crumpled around his waist he couldn't get into the pockets for his hat and gloves. He put his hand on the door handle then hesitated. He sat back in the seat. "What are we supposed to do now?"

"Find out what it is. At least see if we can figure it out." She stared at him from across the car. She still held the baby like that—as if she could protect it from everything that lurked out there in the blackness.

"Well, why don't you put the baby down for one second and give me a hand? You know as much about this stuff as I do."

"All right, but his name is not 'the baby.'" She didn't say it angrily, but more as a mother would talk to a child. She did not move to put the baby down.

"I know."

"Well, what is it then?"

"I know his name. He just hasn't grown into it for me yet. You're the only one with the name. Sally."

"You'll get work, Frank. You've just got to stop worrying about it. That'll make all the difference."

"I know that. You know, though, I never thought it could be better than when it was just you and me."

"It always gets better."

"But we're at the end of everything, Sally."

"That just puts us at the beginning of everything else, doesn't it?"

"I guess it might. But seriously . . ."

"Seriously? Who told me five minutes ago that I was watching an upside down meteor shower?"

Frank chuckled. He reached across the car for her hand. "We're out of money, out of work," he tapped her hand against the car seat, "and out of our minds."

"Isn't it exciting?"

"Exciting? No. I hadn't thought of it like that."

"I have. It's the only way we can."

"Maybe so," Frank murmured. He pulled on the door latch and said, "Wish me luck," before he opened the door. Then he moved quickly out of the car and shut the door behind him as fast as he could so the cold wouldn't get in.

He fumbled with the hood latch, the cold of the grill stinging his fingers. When he opened it and the big springs had locked the hood upright he did not look under it. He had no idea what he was supposed to be doing out here. He'd exhausted his expertise opening the hood.

When Frank did look at the engine it was pitch black, like everything else, except for the small patch of ruddy glowing. Frank stared at it stupidly for a moment then reached his hands out to it and held them over the glow for its warmth.

The car rocked slightly and then the engine died and he knew Sally had turned it off. Through the muffling of the glass he heard the baby begin to cry. He stared at the car's one light, the only point in the world now to hold him. He had never seen blackness like this anywhere. Frank took a deep breath and shouted, "Turn off the headlight."

Its filament glowed for an instant then went dark and Frank could have been any place in the world. He listened to the crying and thought of walking perpendicular to the road until he was gone. He'd be sure to walk into something though. But the black was so complete it was like being weightless. He felt as if he would be as likely to find himself walking into the sky as walking into a tree.

The car rocked again and the door hinge screeched as Sally got out. The door slammed behind her and the baby's cries were muffled again. A flashlight's beam brought the world back, and Frank was glad it was too late to escape.

Sally stood next to him and caught him warming his hands over the disaster. She laughed when she saw that. A moment later so did Frank. She shined the light on the engine and said, "So that's the engine, huh?"

"I think so. Unless this is the trunk."

"No. This has to be the engine. My clothes are in the trunk."

"That's right." Frank couldn't keep it up. "Something's burned out, Sally," he said.

Sally set the worn owner's manual on the edge of the fender. Frank stood next to her and she put her arm around him as they flitted through the pages. "I didn't realize it was so cold out here," she said.

"There," Frank said when they found the drawing of the engine.

They followed the outlines back from the radiator and had a sinking feeling when they concluded that their alternator had destroyed itself. Frank had had that replaced once before. He knew it kept the battery alive. Then Sally turned the drawing over and said, "No, it's on the wrong side. Look."

They retraced the drawing from the radiator, Frank touching the fan belts and following them to their ends. "You're right. The alternator's still here. But we're one belt short."

Sally started to giggle. She stopped a moment, held the drawing next to the fading glow, traced it with her flashlight and started laughing outright. She flicked the light off and hugged Frank hard, turning away from the car. They slid down the grill until they were sitting on the frozen ground, both of them laughing now. Frank wanted to stay this way until daylight, if only because for once she was holding him and ignoring the baby's senseless crying.

"Did you see what it was?" she asked.

"Nope."

"Then why are you laughing?"

"Because you are."

"How do you know I haven't just lost my grip? I could be in the middle of a breakdown."

"That'd be fine. I'd break down with you. It'd be like a vacation."

"It's the air conditioner," she said, nearly cackling. "Our air conditioner melted down when it's ten degrees out."

"Well, we'll miss that."

He hugged her until the laughter stopped. He could still hear the baby whimpering and finally he said, "The baby is crying."

"Oh, it's good for him now and then," she said. Frank hugged her so tightly she complained.

"He's probably cold. I am," Frank said.

"We'll get the car going again to warm him up. I'll take care of warming you up."

They stood up still holding each other. "Dark as a pocket out here, isn't it?"

"You'll love him, Frank. As much as I do."

"I know. I just thought it would be automatic."

"Nothing is. But don't worry about me. I'll always love you the most."

"Then I wasted a wish."

"Not me. You're going to be such a good father."

Sally turned the flashlight off and they stood a moment more, floating together in the darkness. When Frank opened the door at last, the light came on and the warmth from inside poured out to them. Sally got in and he closed the door behind her. He was alone in the darkness again and he ran blindly around the car and fumbled in his haste to get his own door open.

Storm Clouds

The water trailing from the bellies of the startled ducks dotted out a broken vee on the glassy lake and Sam wished he'd always thought that was the most beautiful thing in the world. He watched the birds, their forewings flashing white as they wheeled around the point and out of sight. It had been a long time since he had noticed them. When they were gone he stepped into his cabin and threw Alix's letter and the reply he had been working on into the fire.

He walked back down to the dock then and flipped his canoe right side up and slid it into the water. There were storm clouds building to the west, beyond the far end of the small lake, but this side of the mountains. They would just have to hold off, he thought. He had planned on fishing today. He had planned on it before he ever saw Alix's letter or those dark, billowing clouds.

Sam pushed off and started to paddle, looking away from the spinning rod in the bottom of the canoe. He felt like fishing as much as he felt like seeing Alix. But it had taken him a long time to rebuild even this simple routine, and he was not going to let her steal it away again.

At the peak of his affair with Alix, when it went public and he didn't care, Sam had decided fishing was a vainglorious waste of time. There'd been a pack of them running together then and they'd been tarpon fishing in the Keys when Sam announced this new insight. They had laughed at him, and, full of rum, he had given Alix his father's fly rod to prove how serious he was.

Sam picked up the old spinning rod and cast the heavy spoon, whipping the rod like a lash. The shameful things had piled up so quickly at the end he'd forgotten to be ashamed for throwing away fishing. And his father's old bamboo rod.

He just glimpsed the last of the cast, the spoon splashing down at the end of the arc of line, and the sun catching each ring of the disturbance on the slate smooth water. He paddled hard to keep the lure out of the weeds, fighting the lake with the muscles in his back and arms. He kept paddling that way long after it was necessary.

Sam glanced to the storm, the clouds nearly black at its heart. Alix had the blackest, softest hair he had believed possible. "Black silk," he had said once, toying with it while he thought she slept. He remembered how the front of his thighs touched the back of hers when they slept like that and he understood he would never forget the days she had replaced everything else he knew. With his face inside that raven hair everything had felt so safe and true, when nothing could have been more transient.

Sam paddled hard, watching the front edge of the storm cross the valley, erasing the mountains beyond. The surface of the lake was picking up a riffle now and then, out near the middle. The storm began to tug at the canoe's bow and Sam couldn't remember any other coming in so fast. Suddenly the entire lake was moving, the reflections and the shine burred off by the wind.

Sam swung into the brief protection of a cove and paddled on. He glanced down at the rod which trembled vacantly against his hard, white thigh. Somehow she had heard he was back with his wife. She said she thought that was cute. She actually wrote that, Sam thought, that it was cute. Then, in the next sentence, she said she had also heard he would be at his cabin this week and she was coming to meet him. Sam had no idea how she knew these things about him. It had been impossible to find and sever all the connections from that time.

The torn, leading wisps of clouds were over him now. Behind that the roiling clouds lost their shape in the heavy, gray body of the storm. Billowing cumulus still showed north and south, with the sun slanting below them, lighting the whitecaps outside the cove.

Even as the storm blotted out the last of the sun, Sam turned his canoe toward the whitecaps. He always fished the beaver lodges on the far side of the lake and he guessed he still had the time to cross if he moved fast enough. After the affair, during the rebuilding years, he had learned to cling to routine like a drowning man to a last floating scrap of debris.

He paddled steadily, steeling himself for the moment when he left the cove. Then he was out and the wind slashed at his bow and Sam dropped to his knees, battling back with long, sweeping strokes.

He was out on the real lake now, and it was not the lake he had always known. The canoe wasn't even quartering on the swells. It slid crookedly off each wave and was slapped by the next as it wallowed. The wind made Sam's small diggings with the paddle seem ridiculous.

The first water slipped quietly in over the right side, just a larger wave slapping him during a wallow. It ran down and touched his knees, shocking him with its coldness. He stopped paddling for a moment and studied the water, wondering how it could be so clear in the bottom of his canoe, so leaden and frothed outside.

Another wave hit him just as it broke. It came in over the gunwale, across his hip. His breath was stung out of him, but he started paddling again immediately. He noticed the faded lifejacket tucked uselessly under the front seat and he cut his angle across the lake, giving up some of the opposite shoreline before he ever got there. The waves didn't hit him so hard as he slid off them.

The canoe was beginning to smooth out when a very large wave came over the stern, splashing Sam in the back. He looked over his shoulder, barely recognizing his lake. He gave up.

Glancing to the beaver lodges dotting the bank he couldn't reach, Sam turned directly away from the wind and ran with it, back toward his cabin. The wind kept the canoe moving fast enough to troll and he leaned back, holding the paddle as a rudder. He couldn't do any good out this deep but he was scared now, and he didn't want to stop his steering even long enough to reel in his line. The wind swept away the cold sweat that had covered him when the water had started to come into his canoe and Sam shivered. He measured the distance back home and looked to the sky.

With his rod held under his legs, his knees told him of the strike first. He froze for a moment, then dumbly picked up the fiercely resisting rod. With the rod in his hands, the drag spinning line out, he laughed as wildly as the fish had struck.

The storm swept away his laugh and Sam dropped the drag down a notch. The wind was going to make the fight nearly impossible. He couldn't paddle against the wind and fight the fish as he should. Already his canoe was twisting toward the waves that were now much taller than it was.

He let the fish have its way, only keeping the line taut, but the storm shocked the initial rush out of the old trout. They were far downwind from where the fish had struck and the canoe began to wallow once again.

He knew the fish was large. He pictured the ruddy gill plates, and the slash under each jaw, maybe the jaw even hooking a bit, and he felt sorry for the fish, knowing something so powerful would never have known this kind of impotence.

Sam started to reel in as the waves shuddered against the canoe. They came into the canoe each time now, and the cold was no longer shocking. The fight was down to the fish holding sideways to the pull. He had torn the trout out of his home and now he was hauling him sideways through the rolling lake. He wished his line would break.

A large, spumy wave crashed into the canoe, forcing Sam to leap to the opposite side. The clear, cold, water began to make its own waves inside his canoe. Another wave rocked the canoe and then another, even larger. Sam reached to break the fish off but he pictured the trout, sitting heavy on the quiet bottom, down by the head, chewing at the leaden sharpness in his jaw. They said a fish could chew through a hook, but he didn't know if that was true. He wondered if they could find their way back home.

Crouching lower in the heavy canoe, Sam watched the waves and rocked the upwind gunwale away from each one. He cranked the reel handle faster.

The fish broached in a wave trough beside the foundering canoe and, seeing what lay beyond the water, dove with what was left of its strength. Sam raised the rod tip cruelly but there was only a swirl of lightening green where the fish had been.

The fish dove under the canoe and Sam lunged around after it. The wave hit as he shifted his weight. The canoe listed crazily and Sam dropped to the bottom, rolling to the highside, fighting to bring it down before the canoe capsized.

The canoe levelled for an instant and Sam struggled up. He fumbled with the rod until he had the line in his numbed hands. He tugged at it until it broke.

The trout did not instantly recognize its freedom. It lay on its side in the lee of the canoe, the red and white spoon hanging from a long rip in its mouth, and Sam stared. It righted itself slowly, then, with an exhausted turn of its tail, began the long descent.

The spare paddle, floating on the water inside his canoe, bumped against Sam's thigh. He looked at it stupidly then snatched at it. Staying low in the canoe, he swept the paddle around, almost overturning in the last wave to hit him from the quarter.

When Sam finally straightened to the wind, the water that filled the canoe rolled fore and aft as the waves outside swept its length. He stared at the lureless rod beneath the water and pictured the trout on the bottom with that great heavy lure dangling from its mouth. "You coward!" he yelled, turning to the tempest, and slamming the paddle against the gunwales.

The wind tore at him and the rain finally let go. He watched it pock the water in his canoe and he lowered his head and began to paddle slowly back to his dock.

When the canoe ground against the shore, water surged over the deck plate, then back, washing over Sam. He forced his stiffened legs over the side and he splashed to shore, wrestling with the canoe, finally tipping it and dragging it onto land.

He stood on shore, the wind flattening his sodden clothes, and gazed at the jumbled lake. Uninvited, the memory of the Keys charged into his head—the tickling run the sand made as the sun dried it against his skin, and the rum with its own tickling runs, and his hand lazily on Alix, the startling whiteness of her untanned areas fading as she let the sun work them.

Sam shook his head. He did not plan on remembering her that way. When he had read her letter he had done so with disgust, and he tried to bring that back now, but even then he had known the disgust was hiding the excitement that always ran underneath, like a smooth, warm, underground current.

Sam squinted against the wind and looked to the point the ducks with the white wings had disappeared beyond this morning. "Widgeon," he mumbled, remembering how, when they were first married, he'd told Peg that flocked up and flying as one they were the prettiest thing in the world.

He left the canoe at the end of the drag mark it'd made as he pulled it from the lake. It would be all right there. He crouched down low enough to pick up the fishing rod and he carried it to the cabin and locked it inside. Then Sam walked around the cabin, keeping his hand on its logs for support until he reached his car.

He drove down the rutted drive past the willow-choked outlet stream and on, miles farther, to the highway. He tried to think of himself as virtuous for avoiding Alix, but he couldn't even pretend to that. He was afraid of her now.

He was as afraid of her as that fish would be of the tantalizing red and white spoon, if it could ever really be rid of it, and then after that, if it could find its way back home.

It was seven hours back to his wife, but seven hours was nothing compared to how far from home he had been before, with Alix. And though he could not quite shake the picture of her, with him, on those sweaty, sandy stretches, Sam knew he did not have the courage, or the ruthlessness, to travel such distances again.

Jump Shooting

Harold edged toward the pond, crouching in the open places despite the darkness. After fifty years of duck hunting he still was not sure whether the birds could spot an approach in the dark. Today he would not chance it. He hesitated in the last wrinkle of hill before the unprotected stretch to the reeds and caught his breath. Then he crouched lower than ever and shuffled to the cover of the reeds and sat down. He heard the movement on the water and rested his shotgun on his knees to wait for daylight.

It was cold out, not bone-chilling, but frosty, and Harold imagined the way the sun would feel when it came up, if it was given time to strengthen. He rubbed at his knees which hurt with the cold and the awkward hunched over walk. It was the water that did that. Water and plain old age. Water in this pond and countless others, none like any other, but all with the ducks, or at least the promise of them.

As he rubbed at the soreness Harold recalled the icebreaking retrievals; from pushing the slushy beginnings away to the actual hammering of three-quarter-inch sheets with his gun butt. Mostly though it was just cold water, before the ice had quite formed, that the ducks fell into and had to be gotten out of. He knew only a dog could have saved his knees from that and he smiled because that reminded him of Helen, as nearly everything did since she had gone.

118

They had had a dog for two days. She bought it for him and it had been more than they could afford, but she said she knew he would need a good one and that it would save him from rheumatism. They'd been in their early twenties then and they had laughed at the thought of needing to be saved from anything. They'd also laughed at the beginning of her allergic reaction to the dog. The running nose and red eyes were something she would get over, she said. But when Harold woke to find her gasping for breath, her face purple with the effort to get the smallest bit in, he had picked her up and carried her out of the house and held her in his arms until her breathing eased. Harold never told her, but he had never been as scared as he was that night, carrying her through the back door, bumping her cheek on the casing because she was too weak to hold her head upright.

Harold listened to the feeding murmurs of the ducks, hidden by the darkness and the reeds, and pictured them in those first rays of light when the gun would go off. The first rush into the air would be furious: leaps straight off the water, blurred wings slapping the pond once and the water dragging back off each bird as if unwilling to let them go. Their necks would be strained forward, pulling, anywhere for an instant, before the heads began to swivel and the flock closed and tried to find where the danger lay. Then, with the birds closing on one another, the business of retreat would begin. But it was the moment of the jump, that mix of panic and grace that Harold wished he could see once more.

Harold touched his shotgun, very lightly running his fingers down the furrow between the barrels. He shivered. Her ribs, that night of the choking, had grooves between them that his fingers had slipped into as he carried her. And the strength in those muscles, cording beneath his fingers as they strove for something they had never had to strive for before, seemed suddenly like a weakness, a foreshadowing of a flaw that would show itself later. And it had, of course. He pushed away the last days of her constricted breathing and the labors of those same muscles that no longer held even the memory of strength, though his fingers fit between them as always as he held her and held her.

His shotgun was one of the few things that he had from the time before Helen. Without looking he could see the silver of the receiver where his hand had worn away the blueing and the scratches and the small split in the stock at the butt plate. It was the only one he had ever owned and Helen had never wanted one for herself. She did not like the killing and though she listened when he explained about the jump she had teased him for taking it so seriously. He had gone on, groping for words he had never thought out, about the search for a target in the bursting flock and the swing on that single target through the bedlam of the wings and the water rising and falling at the same time. There was more motion in one instant, he had said, than an eye could comprehend, yet still, if everything was right, the shot connected. It was all for those moments of separating himself from the chaos and swinging smoothly on a single piece of that commotion and bringing it down. It was not the killing. The bird was only proof that he had done what he doubted he was capable of. She'd laughed at the end of the only speech he had ever made and he had never mentioned it again.

She'd tried to soothe him after she realized the hurt and told him it was a good way for them to have some time apart so they wouldn't get tired of each other. But he had never wanted time apart from her, from practically the first time he had met her. And now that they were apart he knew he had been right in never wanting it.

She would understand that, he told himself again. He fingered the checking on the stock and thought of her anger. What he would do was a sin, a terrible one. And although the religion had always meant more to her, he had done more than go through the motions. She had kept it with her through all of it, but the weeks and months of her dying had ground it out of him as surely as the life was ground out of her. There was no God in the world that would've done that to Helen. The thought that the easiest sin of all would keep them from being together forever was too preposterous to bear and Harold slapped the stock of his shotgun with his fist.

The murmur on the pond ceased and Harold sank further into the reeds. He pictured the necks stretched at attention, the feeding stopped, the heads turning, and he did not breath. Finally there was a harsh quack and he was afraid they had started to flush but the sounds of feeding resumed and he let out his breath.

If they were barred from heaven, he thought, or wherever they were bound, that would be too bad. But they would make a hereafter for themselves if they had to. That was the way they had done everything always. He had not the slightest doubt that they would be together again in some kind of afterlife. There would have been no sense to anything if there was not that.

Harold checked the eastern ridge of hills knowing there could not be much time left. The few wisps of clouds were tinged rosy now and the horizon was light. It would be a clear, warm day once the sun was well up and Harold smiled. Only the decoy men needed the snow and rain. If you were willing to walk and crawl he thought, with some of the old pride, any kind of weather was duck hunting weather.

He shifted his weight in the cold reeds and listened to the ducks babble and watched the approach of the sun. The ducks were restive now, the chuckles being replaced by quackings and splashings. He knew the wheat field they would move to when the sun was up and he had come early enough to be with them before then.

The broken ridge of hills in the east was lighted now and Harold judged the brightness, hoping he had lined it up so the sun would come through the notch and touch him and the ducks first. It was silly, all this planning, but, in truth, it was far from the easiest sin, and Harold had known he'd need this routine and this schedule for courage. And now, as the sky lightened and the time grew shorter, Harold began to fear Helen's anger. The trigger motion and the fire would be nothing. He was even curious about it, wondering about the pain and how long it would last. He couldn't imagine Helen would turn away from him as a mortal sinner but the thought tormented him and he could keep it at bay less and less as the dawn unfolded.

There was a brightness now in the bottom of the notch and Harold knew that he had gotten it right and that the sun would touch his reeds, gilding them at the moment he would stand up and the ducks would flush and he would see Helen. He shifted his weight, bringing his feet under him in preparation. His hands were clammy on the stock and the barrels of his shotgun. His heart began to beat more quickly and he thought how it was like this on all the jumps he had to wait for.

Crouching up, he peered through the reeds, needing one look. In the grayish light the water was the color of gunmetal, broken into thousands of silvered ridges by the movements of the flock. He clasped the shotgun tighter, feeling the ridges of the receiver and the trigger guard. The ducks were swimming now, aimlessly, waiting, as Harold did, for the sun, and for flight. Harold saw most of the ducks were mallards and he tried to take deeper breaths. He saw a teal and grinned slightly, picturing their broken, headlong flight. Helen would have to understand and forgive him this one transgression, he thought. He knew she would. He whispered her name as he tested his footing one last time.

The upper ridge of the sun crested the bottom of the hill's notch and the light touched the reeds in front of Harold and he hesitated. He knew how Helen would be here, but maybe there were different rules there. If there was a God, and He had allowed Helen to linger so, He could be just cruel enough to keep me from her, he thought. But the sun was on him now and Harold saw a hen straighten her neck and look at him. He took one last breath. He wanted to be the one to flush them.

The ducks burst wildly at the shot, scattering for a moment in all directions because they did not know where the shot had come from. They formed though, around the hen that did know, in the same way that had mystified Harold since his first jump. The moment of panic was gone and now they were simply a flock in retreat, with the stragglers closing. They would circle the wheat fields more diligently now, knowing danger had come so close, but they would land there all the same, as Harold had known they would.

A drake that had flown alone in completely the wrong direction wheeled back over the reeds that had hidden Harold for so long and flared at the last instant, seeing the danger in the reeds. He did not flare much because he was the last duck and the flock was pulling away without him. It was a compromise Harold had seen hundreds of times.

The second shot took the drake full in his breast, knocking loose both the rusty brown neck feathers and the creamy white of the belly. The broken feathers hung in the first shafts of sunlight as the drake folded into the shot and collapsed.

Harold stood, a tremor running through his body. He did not trust himself to take a step and he watched the duck, head down in the pond, with the silvered rings dying out around him.

The pond was completely still before Harold moved. The sun was on him but it would be some time before it gave warmth. He had little need of that now, though he kicked gingerly through the reeds and stepped into the water. The pond surface broke, and the drake bobbed in the new commotion. The cold bit into Harold as the water went above his knees.

He reached the drake and picked it out of the water carefully, by the bill, so he would not crumple any of the feathers. Water beaded on the tiny, brilliant green feathers of the head, holding itself in small, sparkling spheres. Harold stared at that and at the precision of each feather blending into the next in the perfect pattern, as if he had not seen it thousands of times before. He held the duck against himself, brushing the water away, and he stared into the sun, squinting against the painful glare.

If that was where God truly lived it was a fitting place, he thought. Harold cursed suddenly. He could not risk the unknown. He had realized that and he had fired the first shot to prove it. He was incapable of taking the chance of losing Helen through some wrong move. And he hated God for that. There were no rules that made sense, not since Helen had been taken. And without those he couldn't even guess what he could not do.

He looked again at the drake, having to blink several times before his vision returned. If there was a God, he wished he would knock him down soon. Harold could not be more alone and he certainly could not be flying in any direction more wrong. He reached the reeds and pushed through them. They rattled, dry and dusty along his legs.

Finally he stood again firmly on shore and he turned to the sun. He stretched his arms out, his old shotgun in one hand, the new drake in the other, and he bared his breast to the sun and dared God to knock him down. But no shot came and after a moment Harold began the long trudge back to his empty house. Helen, he knew, would have plenty to say about this morning. He smiled, thinking of how sheepish he would have to look while she railed at him. Then she would relent and hug him, with that same look of happy surprise she always wore whenever she caught him doing something right.

Bone Yard

Dennis sat in the graveyard at night because of the view. From the jutting thumb where the black spruce turned to white stones he could look over the entire flat below him. In the blackness down there the elk moved, through the walls of willow on the frozen creeks, and through the frost-heaved chaos of the bunch grass. He peered into the featureless blackness, sometimes seeing lights that weren't there, sometimes seeing nothing at all. Dennis sat with his windows down in the bitter cold so he could hear the shots when they came.

Very rarely, three or four times a night, a car would pass on the road that also crossed the flat. He would watch the path of lights, tensing without realizing it. He was the only warden who nighted over with the elk and he did it voluntarily. Every night lately. And he did it from the graveyard.

He knew the people under the white stones didn't mind. And he was fairly certain no one else, anywhere, much cared. They were old stones. His wife, he was sure, was perfectly content to have the bed to herself.

Several times he had waited beyond dawn and then stepped from his truck, leaving footprints in the frost over the dead clover. The most recent stone he had found was over fifty years old. Fifteen years older than he was himself, and already in the frost-covered ground.

Many of the stones were older than that, but none over one hundred years old. It was still young country in some ways. More and more frequently he studied the graves until the sun was up and strong, but without heat. He'd read dead dates until he could look at his watch and be sure his wife and his daughters had left the house for another day.

Some of the graves were close together, a man's name on one, a woman's on the other—same last name. Some of these were flanked with younger stones with more of the same name.

Although Dennis truly did not often think of the graves that surrounded him nightly, when he did he always recalled the tight clusters of similarly named stones. The thought made it hard for him to breath and he would stick his head out the window and gulp, although there was no more air out there than there was right in front of him.

Once it was safe to return home Dennis would pull his truck into his driveway and walk into his house, stiff from the cold and the truck. The coffee his wife didn't finish would be cool in the pot and he would microwave a cup as he undid his gunbelt and set it on the table. He'd add wood to the fire his wife had started and when the microwave dinged he would stand with his back to the woodstove and drink the single cup of stale coffee. Then he would lie down on the couch and close his eyes and pull the afghan over himself. His oldest daughter, the single reason he had married sixteen years earlier, had made the afghan but lost interest and it was not long enough to cover Dennis's feet. He curled fetally and would sleep for three hours before his official shift began. He often went for days now without getting out of his uniform.

Even without the sleep he never had trouble staying awake up on the hill in the blackness. He would shiver under the sleeping bag he draped over his legs and he would watch that vast area he could not see.

Anything could happen down there. Anything at anytime. That there was actually that kind of possibility left in the world kept him awake and even eager. The air, cold and clear, would carry the sound of the shots. And the lights of the poachers, when they came, would bolt out of that darkness like lightning.

Dennis knew they would come, too. The snow would not come, though it was late December and they were already well into the first real cold snap, but the poachers would come. Without the snow there was no tracking and the advantage was theirs and Dennis knew they wouldn't be able to ignore that forever.

He had never before wanted poachers as badly as he did now. With every passing headlight Dennis would hope to see a stop, hope to see the car turn to sweep its lights over the flats and over the elk. Then he would hear the shot he listened for and an elk would die and the poachers would move out across the frost heaves and Dennis would ease out of his truck and move off the grave hill, down through the frozen sage.

On the night that the car finally did stop, Dennis had averaged three hours of sleep a day for nearly a month. His wife, Karen, had stayed home that morning and surprised him when he came in for his cup of coffee and nap. "Find your poachers?" she had asked, without looking up from her paper and coffee.

Dennis stood at the door and then closed it behind him. She was in her winter robe, the blue terrycloth one, and under that she wore her flannel nightgown with the lace collar that closed tight around her neck. Her blond hair was dark, with long, heavy curls from the shower. She was still a pretty woman and Dennis did not look at her for more than a moment.

"Why aren't you at work?" he asked. He poured himself a cup of coffee and put it in the microwave for a minute and a half, without realizing it was already hot.

"I took the day off." She looked up then. "Just to see if you ever came home anymore."

Dennis added wood to the stove and stood with his back to it. He burned his lips on his coffee cup but did not swear or even grimace.

"I did laundry yesterday," his wife said. "Have you given up even changing your underwear?"

Dennis looked at the couch. The too-short afghan was folded over the arm. He never folded it when he left for his shift, but it was always tidied by the time he returned. He tried his coffee again and was able to get some into his mouth, though it was still too hot to taste.

"Why do you sleep on the couch?" his wife asked. She didn't sound friendly, not as if she was concerned with any answer he might give. Dennis said to himself, *Because I don't want to even smell where you have been.* But out loud he said, "I'm tired." It didn't answer anything that lay between them and instead of moving to the couch, he stayed in front of the stove, where he did not have to look at her. He did not want her to watch him as he slept. Not on the couch or anywhere else.

"Too tired to make it to the bed?"

Dennis heard the paper rustle and for an instant he was afraid she was coming to him. It didn't make any sense though, she was no more concerned with how little he was around than she was with where he slept, and she didn't come to him. She went to the couch and sat down where he would have liked to have been lying.

She looked at him for a long time and Dennis finished his coffee. He set his hands on his hips, his right hand riding high over his revolver. He let his shoulders sag and for the first time he felt the weight of the nights in the graveyard bear down on him and he wanted nothing more than to be allowed his nap.

"This morning Debbie asked if we were divorced."

Dennis didn't say anything. It seemed a reasonable question he supposed.

"Julie said, 'Of course not. People who don't see each other don't need a divorce.'" Dennis's wife stared at him. "Wasn't that clever of her. For only being fourteen, to know so much?"

Dennis turned back into the kitchen. He said, "We have brilliant children." He put a second cup of coffee into the microwave and wished he hadn't spoken at all. These things could whirl into fights so quickly they sometimes swept him along before he realized it.

He stood in front of the microwave as if it produced the same kind of heat as the wood stove and he burned himself again with his cup. He could still smell the sharp edges of the cold in the cemetery and he could still see the endlessness of night where anything might happen at any moment. He closed his eyes, but it was not the same blackness, not inside his house.

"I think they would really like to see you," his wife said, not moving from the couch. Her voice was an irritant that never disturbed him when he was really on the hill. She hadn't said that she would like to see him. Dennis nearly smiled. They'd gotten past those pretenses long ago. The inertia was something else though. Something else altogether.

Dennis added cold tap-water to his coffee and drank it all off. He walked around the corner wall and looked at his wife on the couch. She was looking at him, even before he was in sight. "You're not staying nights with a woman somewhere?" she asked, as if the idea was nearly too ridiculous to mention. "You're not going to put yourself through that kind of embarrassment, are you?"

They watched each other as he zipped his coat. The idea was ridiculous. He would die before starting anything like this ever again.

"I'm going to go out and check on some leads," he said.

"Leads into what?" she called after him, and then after he closed the door between them he heard her shout, "Leads into what!" again, but the sound barely came through to him.

Dennis pulled out of the drive and moved back onto the road. The mountains, up high, were sinking deeper beneath the snow, but still nothing would fall down here. He drove out to the mountains on the east edge of his jurisdiction, then turned and headed for the mountains that hemmed in the west. He wished with all his might that Debbie had never happened. Without Debbie there would have been no marriage. What had happened between Karen and him, what had brought Debbie and everything else, would be something he barely remembered by now.

He drove back and forth all day, slowly, seeing nothing that had changed in his area. When darkness came, quickly with the overcast, he stopped at the gas station store, the only building he passed on his rounds. He had to walk around back to the house, where he interrupted the owner at his dinner. He declined the invitation to join in supper, and then declined it a second time. He walked with the owner to his store, where he bought a loaf of bread and two cans of pop.

He loaded his groceries in his truck and drove, never over twenty-five miles an hour, the ten miles to the cemetery. A tree had fallen over the short stretch of abandoned dirt road to the graves and Dennis had to get out and chop one end through with the short ax he carried behind his seat. He dragged the top end just far enough to the side to allow his truck through and proceeded with his headlights off.

Once settled into the yard, Dennis pulled his sleeping bag from the passenger seat and tucked it around his legs. He thought of the graves of the families, so closely placed forever, and he leaned an arm out his window so his shoulder and head were out of the cab. He ate two pieces of bread without bothering to look for the pop that had rolled onto the floor.

The darkness was complete with the overcast that had lasted for days, and after a few hours Dennis began to feel feathery touches of cold against his face. It was snowing and it always gently surprised him that it was impossible to see something as white as snow, no matter how dark it was. Even with a sky full of white, the blackness was unchanged, except for the cold, wet traces on his face.

Dennis did not tense when the first two sets of lights passed that night. They were just lights and he watched the snow caught in them, glad for the chance to be able to see it.

When the third vehicle came into view Dennis saw that the snow had begun to cover the road. The lights were brighter against the snow and Dennis did not notice when the truck first began to slow. But when it was merely crawling along Dennis sat upright, still with his head outside the truck.

The white reverse lights lit a small space immediately behind the truck and the high beams swept slowly across the flats. They jerked to a stop once, then continued before stopping again, just as Dennis had imagined they would.

Dennis eased open his door and left it open, not wanting to worry about any noise from the closing. He had long ago disconnected the wires for the automatic cab light.

Dennis looked away from the truck for an instant, trying to place his feet, but, especially after the light, it was impossible to penetrate the darkness. The shots, fast and light, came before he had lifted his head—three so close together that as soon as the echoes died Dennis was not sure how many there had been. His heart sped and he crouched as he crept down the hill away from the graves, feeling his way with his hands and his shins. He kept his eye on the lights and, when they went off, he kept staring where he remembered them to be. His eyes hurt with the strain of the blackness.

Dennis sat suddenly on the slick hillside and the snow wet his hands. He waited until his breathing eased and then he listened. The lights were gone and the engine down there was not running. There was no sound at all anymore and Dennis waited. He did not begin moving again until the small points of a pair of flashlights began to weave across the frost heaves. They were too dim to show anything to Dennis, other than that they were there.

He edged down the hill again, pushing himself with his hands, sliding on his boots and butt. He never looked away from the lights that way, and he did not worry about falling. He was surprised when he bottomed out in the ditch. In the blackness, with only the dim pricks of lights out in the flats, a vertigo had come over Dennis. He stood to a crouch and found it hard to believe he was at the level of the road.

The lights in the field were no longer moving. Staying in the ditch and moving until the lights were blocked, Dennis found the truck. He crossed over to it and by using the background of the flashlights he saw that the bed was empty. He moved up to the cab and through the drawn up window he saw the silhouette of a head behind the wheel. By the hair he knew it was a woman and he squatted on the snow-covered pavement then crabcrawled backwards to the ditch he had just left.

In the dense quiet of the light snowfall Dennis could hear the men in the frost heaves working. Even their breathing came to him, hard and in gasps, depending on the breeze. He heard a saw work quickly against bone.

Dennis had expected a chain saw. The poachers working for the profit of the antler trade were pros who rarely stayed in the field more than a minute—just long enough to cut the antlers, and maybe the ivories, and run. Simple meat poachers rarely worked at night but, listening to them panting out there in the darkness, Dennis guessed they were bringing in the whole animal. That was not what he had expected.

Dennis shivered in the ditch and the longer the men stayed in the field the more certain he became that they were simply stealing food. A pro's truck would have kept going, then come back and picked them up when they were done. A parked truck at two A.M. at five degrees below zero was suspicious in itself.

When he heard the men dragging something large toward the truck Dennis crouched up on the balls of his feet and put his hand on his revolver. The tailgate banged down and he heard one of the men say, "For Christsakes, give us a hand."

The domelight came on then and Dennis lay down in the ditch. For a moment he could see the two bundled-up men, tipping the back half of an elk onto the tail gate. The woman was thin, even through her clothing, and one of the men told her to close the door. The light snapped out when she did.

"Come on," one of the men said, breathing so hard Dennis worried about him. Then they all moved away from the truck and Dennis listened to them begin dragging in the other half. For an instant all sorts of plans leapt into his head: stealing their car keys, driving their truck away, drawing his revolver and crying *Freeze!* Dennis had never once, in fifteen years, drawn his revolver. Then he heard them laughing for a short moment, all three of them, the two men and the woman, enjoying some joke he hadn't been able to hear. He lay in the ditch while they loaded the last half of the elk.

He studied their cold, tight faces in the brief moments of the cab light and, when the headlights came on, he read the license number on the truck. He watched the truck drive away then, the snow falling thickly enough now that they tried the high beams once, but lowered them back to normal to avoid the glare off the flakes.

When they rounded the hills and even the glow of their lights on the sky had disappeared, Dennis groped his way back up to the cemetery, stumbling in the impenetrable darkness, where he had always felt that there was a possibility of anything happening next.

As soon as he sat down in his truck he was exhausted. He brushed snow off his legs and tucked the sleeping bag back around them. He shook his hat off, outside the open window, then put it back on and leaned his head against the rear window of his truck. He closed his eyes and then opened them. It was the same view either way and he left his eyes open.

It was never the poachers he was after. He wanted the possibilities the empty darkness had held, and now they had left him too. It was just darkness after all, and he was the same in the darkness as he was in the light and he had done nothing but sit in the ditch with the snow piling up on him watching all the possibilities drain away.

He sat the rest of the night with his eyes open and when the dull gray streaking began to open up the east he reached for the ignition and turned on his truck. He drove slowly around the tree he had cut the evening before and out onto the asphalt, which was hidden now beneath the snow. He was the first person to cut a track through the clean snow and it led to his house.

His wife's car was in the driveway and there were not yet any tracks from the school bus. But there were lights on in the house and he saw his wife move in front of the kitchen window as he sat in his truck taking deep breaths. He had not closed the windows on the drive home, or even turned on the heater and his face was red and pinched, his whole body drawn up against the cold and the exhaustion.

As he walked through the snow to the front door he wished it did not stay dark so late in the winter. If he could have caught them still in bed, and awakened them, it would have been so much easier. They would have been disoriented and not sure of anything he said and he could have been gone before any of the fighting swirled round him.

He opened the front door and the heat rushed out at him and even before he turned toward the kitchen he heard his oldest daughter call out, "Well, look who's here."

He stepped into the edge of the kitchen and looked through it to where they all sat at the table, stopped over their breakfast, as if they already knew something had changed. He pulled his shoulders even tighter toward his neck and he did not unzip his jacket or take off his heavy mittens or fur hat.

"Come home for Christmas, Dad?" Julie asked, smiling, but already with that tone her mother could use, making the least vicious things sound different.

Dennis realized he didn't know when Christmas was. He foundered for a moment, looked toward the microwave for the time. His wife said, "It's the first day of the vacation, Dennis. Are you going to join us? Going to give the poachers a break?"

Dennis hated that she could see through him like that, that she could tell the first moment he was off balance. He looked into the three faces, so much alike. He rubbed at his face with his mittened hand, wondering what in the world it looked like now. He could hear the whiskers scratch against the leather.

"Which one of you wanted to know if your mom and I were divorced?" he said, his voice strange after the long, silent night. He saw Debbie look down at the table and Julie glance to her mother. Karen's gaze did not flicker from his face.

"Which one?" he asked again.

"She was only kidding, Dad," Julie whispered.

Dennis looked at all three of them again and knew they had not just paused in their breakfast, but that they were finished with it now and that he had done that.

"Well, we are divorced," Dennis said. "Finally." His daughters were both staring at their plates now, and Dennis watched them, only looking close enough to his wife to see that she did not drop her gaze.

"It'll be official as soon as it can happen, as soon as the lawyers do . . ." Dennis didn't know anything about that end of it, and it didn't matter anyway. He was only a few feet from the door and he took a step back toward it.

"This won't change much of anything for you. It's been the same way for so long." Dennis put his hand on the doorknob, for an instant wondering what he should take with him. He had not planned for this at all. He opened the door as soon as his wife started to speak. It didn't matter what he left.

"Don't say anything, Karen." He looked at her for the first time, actually meeting her eyes. "Can't you imagine what a relief this will be?"

She didn't say anything then and Dennis looked at his two girls who continued to look at the table. "Maybe I'll come visit," he said, "for the holidays," though he knew it would be a lot longer than that before he would come back. He wondered if he ever would. They didn't say anything and he stepped back outside, where the snow was falling at the same easy pace.

He walked through the gentle touches of the white and climbed back into his truck. He started out toward the cemetery, but it was fully light now and he had never been there during the day. He didn't know where to go.

Broken Flock

My folks never could make a go of it. That's the first thing I ought to say. And I don't think my dad ever really pulled out of it. Probably because it was mostly his fault. My mom did fine. There were no big scenes or anything. One day she figured out she had married a man who was supposed to live alone. I think my dad knew that about himself too, or figured it out soon after, but even for him, that wasn't a comfortable thing to realize.

She moved to California when I was seven and I went with her, of course. You hear all about the turmoil and the poor kids of broken homes nowadays. But back then, for me anyway, it was no big deal. My dad wasn't that big a thing to me. And besides that, we lived in Montana. I don't know if you've ever been there, but it's not like here. That place is where they invented the boondocks. We lived there because my dad grew up there and owned the land. It was on the Missouri River, in the middle of nothing, but it had a lot of sloughs and ponds on it. That brought in the ducks and held them. And they held my father like chains. So when we moved to California it was just kind of like "see you around." Like I said, there were no big scenes or anything.

We live up north of San Francisco, right near the ocean. Practically next to Point Reyes. My mom married a doctor, so he could fork for the land no problem. He's all right, but he works like a dog so he's not around all that much. Now that I can drive, I'm not around much either. In fact, he may be around a lot more now. I'm not there enough to know. He and my mom are pretty tight. Could be he worked like that to sock away a good roll of cash they could have after I was gone. You see, it'd be wasted time for him while I was there anyway. Who wants to bring up somebody else's kid? So why not work all that time, then be able to kick back once I was out of the way? That just occurred to me. That's probably what's going on. It's what I'd do.

Now that I'm driving I go down to the Reyes most of the time. It's winter now and hardly anyone goes there. A couple of surf casters, mostly Viets or Koreans or whatever they are, and a few rangers is all. So I've got the dunes and dune grass and most of all that beach and rock to myself.

But what got me going on all this, about my dad especially, is the ducks. This time of year you can hardly see some patches of the water because they're so thick. I watch them a lot, when I find a good place to sit out of the wind. The dune grass is real rough and it saws together over your head when the wind whips it around. I listen to that and watch the black flocks—they call them rafts—bob around out there like there wasn't a two-flag wind and the rollers weren't six feet tall.

The damp soaks through my pants and at my elbows if I sit in one place too long. That's when I start to wonder about hunting them. If you've ever hunted ducks you know why being damp and cold would make you think that way. My dad took me duck hunting every time I visited him, so I know. I don't know what kind of ducks these are, but I call them all Oldsquaws, because I like that name.

My dad would know what they really are. All he knows about is ducks. He might even know how to hunt these. I'm not sure. I don't think he's ever been out of Montana. I've thought about bringing him here sometime. I'd like to see his face when he saw those ducks out past the surf.

He'd never come down though. Every time I ever saw him, after moving down here, was back up in Montana. I'd fly in and he'd take me back to the house by the Missouri. Every fall for quite a while, though it's been a few years now. I guess my mom's going to wait till I ask to go. He'd never ask. And when he sent me back here with that old shotgun last time, my mom wasn't any too excited to send me back up. She'd taken it off the carousel in the airport. Even in the box she'd known what it was. She put it in her closet in her bedroom without opening it. She said that wasn't going to happen to me too. Now she stacks her shoes on it. She'd have a fit if she knew I took it out sometimes. I've even brought it down here and sat in the dunes with it. Not that I could shoot anything. I don't even have any shells.

The gun's got two barrels, one next to the other one. The inside of the barrels are smooth, like mirrors. It smells too, like my dad's hands always did. The wood is dark and the grain takes a big swirl right where the bend is, before it widens out to fit on your shoulder. I still can't believe he gave it to me.

The first time I went to Montana and he let me carry a gun I think I was around ten years old. I'm not sure. I can never remember things by how old I was when they happened, like some people can. I just remember what happens. He woke me up in the dark, like he always did, by wiggling my toe through the blankets. I must have been around ten, because I know it wasn't legal for me to hunt yet. Things like that never concerned my dad at all.

I looked at the frost on the windows as I ate my oatmeal. Then we left the house and my nose pinched shut and stayed that way, like it was frozen together. I remember wondering how I would thaw it out, if I'd have to stick it in the bathtub or what, and if I'd be able to hold my head under water long enough for it to unfreeze, when my dad handed me a shotgun.

At first I just looked at it, like he was going to show it to me. Then he jiggled it at me, for me to take it. I did. It was heavy and pressed my mittens against my hands and I knew that would make them get cold faster. It wasn't even light out yet, but I was used to that. We did the same thing every morning. We started to walk to the river and he said, "They'll all be on the river. The cold snap's got all the ponds frozen."

I nodded in the dark like I knew and started to point the shotgun at things we walked by, from the hip, like they do on TV. He must've seen that. He said, "There's nothing in that gun. It's not loaded."

I stopped pointing it then. It was a pretty dumb joke.

"When you show me you're not going to kill me, I'll give you some shells."

I didn't say anything. I didn't know why he thought I'd want to kill him. I hardly even knew him. Then he said, "Don't point it unless you're going to shoot. Ever."

I tried to hold it without pointing it at anything but it had to point somewhere. By the time we reached where we had to crawl to his blind I was sweating thinking it might explode. It seemed like it pointed everywhere at once. When we got in I put the gun down and sat on the cold wooden bench with my back to it.

It was getting light enough to see, but nothing happened. I was blowing my breath onto my mittens, watching how the frost stuck on the end of each little wool hair. The honking took a second to sink in, then I lifted my head because it seemed like something you couldn't help listening to. It wasn't a normal honking, like geese. It was something more than that. It was birds talking, and it's still the only time I've heard that.

My dad smiled. It was light enough to see that. "Whistlers," he said. "Swans." He listened for a moment more then said, "They're about a mile up. Moving south."

Then he picked me up and carried me out of the back of the blind very carefully and squatted next to me so he was as tall as I was. He pointed straight up and the canvas of his worn out hunting jacket scraped my ear. I followed his arm up, past the outstretched finger that he didn't even have a glove on, and then way, way past that. Then, past that even, I saw them. They were so high the sun was on them when it wasn't even near to touching us. They were stretched out in vees, long ones, but all lopsided, with one leg longer than the other. I remember wishing they could have gotten the vees straighter. They were just tiny arrows of birds and they were a mix of red and pink, the way the sun was hitting them. For a long time I thought they were always that color.

But there was a rush of something through the air above our heads then and he jumped back into the blind, still holding me. I'd done this often enough to know the ducks were coming in.

He handed me the empty gun again and I had to take it. I pointed it at the front wall of the blind, angling it up at the space he shot through.

"When I say so," he said, "We'll stand up and you pick out a duck, which ever one is closest to you. Point the gun at him and follow him with it."

He straightened in his crouch so he could see over the wall and then said, "Now."

I stood up and started to raise the gun. There were five ducks coming in, all with their wings making those upside down U's. Sliding down and at us. But I didn't point the gun. My dad's went off and I'm sure a duck fell. He hardly ever misses. But I was staring at the front wall of the blind. He'd torn it down. You could still see the damage, and I knew right away he'd done it so I would be able to see over it to shoot when I stood up. I looked at him just as he dropped another duck with his second barrel. That he'd actually torn down his blind for me surprised me more than anything he'd ever done in my life.

He looked at me with the look he always had after he shot and killed. Glazed kind of, but happy and sad all at once. "Why didn't you shoot?" he asked, but I knew he wasn't back yet. Those ducks would still be coming at him for another second or two.

I waited, then said, "My gun's empty."

He laughed then. He dug in a pocket of his vest and handed me two shells. Before he showed me how to load he showed how I should hold the gun and how to look down the barrels without seeing anything but the bead on the very end. Then he loaded it and we sat down and no more ducks came and that shotgun was like holding a snake in my lap. I tried not to move so it wouldn't go off. I kept wishing he would see the ducks and say, "Now," again, so I could stand up and shoot it and have it be empty again.

But no ducks came. He started to talk, whispering the whole time, about different kinds of decoy spreads, and how ducks came in to them, and about jump shooting. That's where you crawl around and surprise them into flying off the water, instead of sitting in a blind and waiting for them to come to you.

Then, in the middle of that dark, moldy blind, he asked, "How's your mother getting along?"

I didn't say anything for a while. He'd never once mentioned her or asked about California since we'd moved away. For a horrible second I thought he might be interested in her again. I had visions of returning to this house forever, of having to take the school bus every morning with my nose frozen together, and having to go duck hunting every day. "She's married," I blurted, then added, "to a rich guy," to let him know it was hopeless. But he just nodded and his eyes switched around the edge of the blind opening, checking for flight.

A duck came in from behind us and landed hard, right in with the decoys, before my dad had a chance to do anything. I could see it swimming around with the wooden ducks and I wondered what it thought about them. The two my dad shot were still floating out there too, upside down. "Are you going to shoot it?" I asked. It was the longest time I'd ever watched a live duck that wasn't out of range.

"It'll help bring in more," he said.

Then I realized I could unload my gun if I shot at this duck. I stood up and peeked at him, starting to point the shotgun in his general direction. "I can shoot him," I said, and I even thought I might have been able to. Watching them when they were flying I'd known I hadn't the slightest chance of even touching one.

My dad took me by the shoulder and sat me down again. "You can't shoot them on the water," he said. "That's as close to the real thing as jerking off." I didn't know what he meant but I was busy again, trying not to let my gun go off.

After a while he asked me how I liked my new dad. I told him I only had one dad. I really felt like I didn't have any dad, but I was feeling mean about telling him Mom married a rich guy. He rubbed my shoulder when I said it, so I was glad I had.

"There were a lot of things your mother couldn't understand about me," he said, his hand still on my shoulder.

"Me too," I said. I meant that she couldn't understand about me too, but it didn't sound like that. He didn't seem to notice. It was true either way I guess.

"She's all right. It was wrong for her to take you though. A boy needs his father a lot more than his mother."

I glanced around the dank blind because I could tell he was looking at me. I never felt like I needed either one of them, especially after my mom got married again. The best thing about my dad was that he didn't treat me like a kid. He treated me like he treated anyone else in the world—almost as if you weren't there. But I couldn't picture living with him without Mom. He'd forget I was there after a while and I'd probably starve. I know that wouldn't have actually happened, but I remember that's what I was always afraid of when I went to visit him.

"I would have stayed married to your mother forever," he said. I could tell he was looking for ducks again, so I picked at the shotgun in my lap. If it went off now it would blow a hole right out of the front of the blind. I pictured how the sticks would fly. "But she just couldn't see things for how they were. She couldn't compromise.

"Maybe marriage wasn't for me. Like she said. But I would have stayed married to her if she hadn't left."

The blind was warming up with both of us in it and it stank. I was glad my mom had left.

There was a whistle of wings overhead and I could see my dad tense and forget what he had on his mind. But the duck flew on and he relaxed. "It's like that duck," he said, his head still turning so slightly to scan the horizon. "Until you get it in range, it's all you can think about. And then when it's yours, for that one second when you stand and shoot, there's nothing better in the whole world. But after that, what is there? Nothing but more plucking and another duck dinner. Do you have any idea how many duck dinners I've had?"

"Plenty," I said.

"You got that right, kiddo." He laughed. "You got that right."

"So how come you keep blasting them?"

"For those couple of seconds. Every time. Just for that." He shook my shoulder again and said, "I knew you'd understand."

I looked at my dad then, to see if he knew who he was talking to.

"When the ponds are open," he said, "maybe next fall when you visit, we're going to go jump shooting. That's what it's really all about. This blind stuff is okay, but it's not jump shooting.

"Blind shooting is like when you've been married just a little while. It's still exciting but all you have to do is sit at home and wait for it. You know they'll come to you sooner or later. And you're already trying not to realize that the thrill won't be able to stand that forever. But jumping, that's everything. You're going out and finding them. Seeing them before they see you and then putting the stalk on them. And if you do everything right they're yours. Then you move on to the next pond. You don't just sit at home and wait for it to come in. That's still good, but just the same as the last one. That's what your mother never could understand."

"Yeah."

"Then, once you get to fighting, and it's no fun anymore but just a job, it's like picking up the dead ones at the end of the day. You can look at them and touch them but you can hardly believe that was what you did everything for. It almost makes you ashamed sometimes."

I just kept agreeing with him all that day, because that was when I figured out that's what I had to do with my parents. It's just easier to agree with them. I still do it most of the time today, with everybody, but now that I can drive, sometimes I just go away. It gets hard on you after a while, always agreeing.

Lying out in the dune grass, with my dad's shotgun, which is illegal here, I try never to think of that part of his talk. Because now I know what he meant. I started to figure it out a few years later, listening to guys at school. And then one day I knew exactly what he meant and that's why I haven't seen him in a few years. It had happened to me the night before at a party with a girl who was almost my friend, but afterwards she wasn't anymore. I didn't like any of it. At all. But I couldn't stop, and neither could she. It's gross, you know. You never want to think of your parents like that.

But I watch the ducks and, though I try to forget he ever said that about my mom and everything, I try to remember all he said about the ducks. There is just no way to get these. I'd like for him to see that. Not to be mean, but just to show him that there are things he was never supposed to have. It's that way for everybody.

I point the gun at those ducks, way out of range out there and safe. He's not getting new girls all the time, I know that. He never once had a girlfriend when I was up there. And he let my mom go just so he could.

He's wrong, you know. I've shot ducks with him. Those two seconds are like he says. I don't like that they are, but it is true. When I stand to shoot and then do it, there is something terrible about it. And the worst is I know I want to do it again.

But he's wrong about after that, when I go to get the ducks. It is something to be ashamed of, but not for why he says so. They're dead and they will never again be anything but dead, and I did that to them for a few seconds of a feeling I can't even describe. And I feel a lot worse than ashamed, but if another one were to fly over at that second, I know I'd drop the dead one and start to swing on the live one to try and hit it too. After I did what I did with the girl who had almost been my friend I felt like that—like when I pick up the dead bird and see what I've actually done. But I did not want to do it again and again like my dad did. He was so wrong about that.

I'd like to creep up the backs of these dunes with him. Make it like we were going to jump shoot the holy hell out of the world's biggest flock as soon as we get to the ridge. Really get him worked up, you know. Crawl so low the sand would stick to our cheeks and the grass would whip over our ears. We'd have to cradle our shotguns in the crooks of our arms and touch the barrels with our faces. Then I'd stop just short and watch his face as he pushes through the last barrier of dune grass and sees all of them out there. "You can't get them," I'd say. "You're not even supposed to have a chance." Not to be mean or anything, but just, for once, to show him.

Mardi Gras

Ron had never been attracted by speed, but with the windy plain's slope down from the mountains, he was running at over one hundred miles an hour. This wasn't fun or thrilling. In fact, it scared him, but he wished he could go faster.

A rocket wouldn't be fast enough of course. He could still see with perfect clarity, and all he could see were her legs wrapped so tightly around a stranger's bare waist. When he had opened his front door his eye had taken it in, but he had backed away before the image could work its way into his brain. Now it would not go away. They hadn't seen or heard him, and he had set his briefcase back down in his Buick and driven away.

After the stop at the bank, where he left the family car, he walked to the import dealer and bought the little Triumph Spitfire he had been driving by for weeks. His hands shook and the man in the lot had to help him lower the ragtop.

Three hours out of Denver the radar detector squealed and Ron cut his speed in half. He snapped off the radio. He would use this time to think. He had to come up with a destination. He would drive into the Atlantic eventually, if he kept on like this.

Seeing the patrol car ahead of him, driving in the same direction,

143

made the first decision easy. Ron took the next exit and worked the Spitfire back up to speed, more gently this time.

Dusk was not far away and he was in Kansas. Kansas for god's sake. It was nearly two hours before he flashed through Oklahoma and into Texas. He had lived his whole life around Denver and had never once set foot in these flat, desolate states. But it made him feel like he was getting somewhere, crossing through Oklahoma in twenty minutes.

It was fully dark now, other than his headlights and the odd light of isolated homes, and Ron slowed under the cover of the darkness. He turned on the radio and chanced upon a live report of Mardi Gras festivities in New Orleans. There would be a crashing finale on Fat Tuesday. Ron could hear the revelry in the background. Instead of remembering coming home early to the surprise, Ron remembered leaving for work that morning and he realized it was almost Tuesday now.

Ron slowed again, enough to keep the map from blowing out of the car. He caught snatches of roads and numbers and turned onto the first road that led in the direction of New Orleans. He stopped for gas when he had to, buying candy bars and chips and sodas for road food. He had never driven like this in his life, but he had heard of younger men doing it and it made him feel that way. Young. He was going to a party and he couldn't even take the time to sleep, he was that wild and that young.

It was something to have a convertible sportscar, he thought. And to be driving at one in the morning in the first week of March with the top down. The south was a good place just for that. The wind, deflecting off his leather flight jacket, had just the right chill to keep him from losing track of the driving.

When he drove fast enough it was as if there was nothing behind him. If he drove far enough, he thought, it might even be like he had never laid eyes on his wife's legs in his entire life. If he got far enough into the French Quarter it might be like being born again, with everything before him instead of behind him.

Whenever he thought about his wife he would turn away from her and drive a little faster, remembering what it was like to be young and going to a party. He had goose bumps under the leather of his heavy jacket. Sometimes he would get as far as to wonder what she was telling their daughters, about where Daddy was. He pictured the traces of fear and doubt that must be eating at her, the slick taste of guilt crinkling and blackening the glossy edges of her successful deceit. But ever since he had decided he was going to Mardi Gras he had been able to funnel his thoughts back to the happy noises of the revelers and he smiled, knowing he would soon join in that.

By dawn Wichita Falls was behind him and he figured if he could average seventy five miles an hour he could be in New Orleans by two in the afternoon. He flicked through the radio stations settling for recorded Dixieland jazz, which he had never listened to before in his life.

They may have found his car in the bank lot by now. When they did she would discover the withdrawal from their savings and she would know she had been caught. As awful as that would be, it would be easier for her to know it absolutely. Ron wished he had been thinking clearly enough to cover his tracks to leave her in doubt a bit longer.

He drove faster as he wondered at how simple he had been for never suspecting a thing. He tried to comfort himself by saying that it wasn't a requirement that he be suspicious. That was not a part of marriage. But her bridge nights, and all her meetings as a realtor danced about before him and it was hard not to see what an incredible dupe he had been. The thought of everyone he knew chuckling over the way his wife spent days grovelling with a stranger almost made him sick.

He flicked through the radio stations again, but couldn't find any more live reports with the happy noises of the crowds. He was sweating from the way he had been thinking and he wriggled out of his jacket, keeping first one hand, then the other, on the wheel while he fought with the binding material. He threw the coat into the narrow slit of the back seat and studied the map again, adding up all the small red numbers alongside his route, detouring around Dallas.

By ten he had side-slipped Shreveport and was in Louisiana. That made four new states for him. A pretty successful trip he decided, for a man who had only been in three states in his entire life. He lay out a course for Baton Rouge and drove on, buoyed up by the new state and the unfamiliar heavy, wet heat spilling past his bug-smeared windshield. He glanced at the bushy trees with their never-ending foldings of greens and darker greens, and thought he might lose himself forever in foliage like that.

He filled up once more in Baton Rouge and climbed stiffly back into the low seat which had already formed to his body. The freeway was on stilts now, riding over a mucky wasteland of black water and gray-green trees that Ron assumed was the bayou.

The traffic clotted near New Orleans and for a long time Ron watched the red reflection of his entire car mirrored at eye level in the hub of a semi wheel. He took the next exit he could.

He had never seen such a confusion of diagonal cross streets, missing street signs, and run-down buildings. He took every street that ran south or east, for as far as it would go, until he was on what would be more accurately described as a trail. Even without his jacket on he was sweating uncomfortably. But he liked the smell of the air; it was full of water and some gentle decay. It was not like the Denver slums. The buildings he drove by were so different, with their porches and scraggling yards, that he wasn't even sure if this was a slum. He had never imagined a slum with palm trees.

Ron came to the Mississippi. He stopped and stared, liking how it moved as if there was nothing else in the world to do. He turned onto a dirt road that followed the river. He couldn't be lost now, with the slow, brown river to guide him. He could almost hear those people hooting and shouting and laughing. He drove slowly along the deserted river, and couldn't help thinking of the quietness that had always surrounded his wife. He had thought it meant that everything was all right. He guessed now that it had probably meant something else.

He had never been wild, and sometimes he thought he had never been young. But his wife had been so soothing and calm, that Ron thought she loved him for his lack of wildness. They never fought. In bed they read to each other. Ron let her have her way and that maintained the calm. Now he wondered if he should have been wilder for her.

He looked at the placid water oozing between the concrete and metal banks, and knew that he was wrong. It was she who had taken her feet off the ground to wrap her legs around something strange and unknown. Ron would have followed the lazy, opaque waters forever.

The quiet died out gradually and Ron saw barricades up ahead. A policeman waved an orange baton at him and Ron followed it to his left. He was the only one following the river in, and the bored policemen kept waving their sticks at him.

Their path led to the Superdome. There was a steady trickle of people pouring from its exits, adding to the throng that filled all the streets to the east. Ron followed the car in front of him and parked next to it in the dark concrete shelter. Two men and two women got out of the car he had followed. They were happy and young and they said hello.

Ron walked down the smooth ramps with them, and they faltered in the brightness at the exit together. But when their eyes adjusted the four young people dashed across the street and, though he tried to follow, they were swallowed by the crowd. So was Ron.

He bustled along, smiling with all these people and the next time he looked up he saw a sign on the boulevard that said Canal Street. There were floats going by and women on the floats threw things into the crowds, plastic bracelets and necklaces and coins. A coin hit Ron in the chest and he caught it before it bounced away. There was a girl pushed against him, who could almost have been one of his daughters. Ron held the coin out to her and she took it from him, smiling. A moment later she held a bead necklace up to him, holding it open with both hands. Ron bowed and she slipped the beads over his head. He felt it there on his neck and said thank you.

Ron bumped through the crowds still dazed from twenty hours in his new car. He laughed out loud when he saw the sign for Bourbon Street. It was nearly impossible to move through the crowds, but everybody was happy and did not mind being nudged back and forth. Ron turned onto Bourbon street, still laughing.

He bought a can of Dixie beer from a street vendor and dropped a piece of the ice that clung to the can down the neck of his shirt. The tingling felt just like he imagined the party would. A block later he bought a T-shirt with a row of leaping jesters across the chest. He unbuttoned his business shirt and stripped it off, letting it drop onto the pavement to be trampled. Someone hooted and clapped him on the back. Ron grinned and pulled the T-shirt over his head. He finished his beer and saw the man beside him squash an empty can on the side of his head. Ron tried it too. It hurt and he laughed again.

The buildings surrounding him had tall, narrow doors and windows and wrought-iron porches on the second story. People spilled from all the windows and all the doors and hung out over the iron railings of the porches. It was as noisy a place as Ron had ever heard. His wife would probably have hated it. But Ron wasn't sure anymore. He pretended that she would, then vowed not to think of her anymore. The noise and the people would definitely frighten his daughters, who were too timid to ever put a necklace around a stranger.

There was a crescendo of laughing and hollering in front of him and Ron followed the crowd's gaze up to see a lacy bra sailing out over the street. A second one followed.

The porch was packed with women, and a few men. The two bra flingers shook slim shoulders and breasts at the admirers below and disintegrated in giggling laughter. Coins and beads showered their section of balcony. One of the women tried to stretch a bracelet around her breast but it snapped off and spun into the crowd. There was a struggle on the pavement for it.

Soon the women forgot the crowd and stood on the balcony, half naked, talking and drinking like anyone else, being occasionally pelted by a handful of beads when someone spotted them for the first time. They would laugh then and wave.

Ron stared at their nakedness, there for everyone to see, then turned suddenly away. He bought another beer and drank it in just a few swallows. His eyes watered with the sting of the carbonation but he was able to look at the women and not see his wife's body in place of theirs. He belched enormously, and someone beside him shouted "Bravo!"

Ron slipped into a bar and the noise of the crowd was drowned by the throbbing of the drums and the blare of the horns.

The black men in the band were all sweating profusely and Ron bought a red drink called a hurricane. It was what everybody was drinking and it tasted sweet and powerful at once. He drank it off and got another. He watched the trombone player's cheeks puff and fall until he was pushed away from the bar.

He was in the swirl of the crowd then and a woman grabbed his arm, took a drink from his hurricane and danced several steps with him before swirling away and repeating her trick with the next man she bumped into. Ron watched her until she was out of sight. He bought one more hurricane, in a plastic cup, and struggled out of the bar. The naked women on the balcony were gone.

Ron started to sip his drink. He was jostled by the crowd and some of the drink slipped over the edge of the cup. He licked at the sticky red juice on his fingers.

He was going to have to slow down, he thought. After the long drive the drink was going to his head. He tried to add up the hours he had been awake, and the numbers lined up like little red mile markers on a map, starting with his wife under a stranger and ending here with a laughing naked woman trying to put a bracelet around her breast. He couldn't add up the tiny red numerals. He said out loud that he had been up for two days and someone toasted to that.

Dusk came and Ron gave himself up to whatever direction the crowd travelled in. The tumult kept increasing. There were people in confusing costumes jostling through the crowds. Ron tried to focus on them but they were too colorful and gaudy. Floats drifted about in the streets, broken away from their designated paths and lost in the unyielding crush of the party.

A man on stilts, dressed like a jester, lurched past and crashed into the crowd. He was caught before he reached their heads and thrown back up to a vertical position. But he couldn't find his legs under him and he crashed again. Ron helped catch him and he heard the man begging to be let down. Ron pushed with everyone else to throw him upright. He fell in the opposite direction and Ron dropped into the wake of a lost float. The people already on it pulled him up and he sat on its edge. Fireworks split the sky but Ron could only see snatches of them between the tall, close buildings.

He lay back on the crêpe paper of the float and watched the flashes of light and bright colors. The fireworks stayed visible on his eye after they had faded and died out. Everything swirled about the bits of color his eyes held, and Ron fingered the necklace around his neck to anchor himself to something. More people were climbing on the float all the time. One of them stepped on Ron and fell over. He crawled back over and grasped Ron's head, laughing and apologizing. He fell off the float when Ron sat up and he lay on the street, laughing until the crowd swallowed him.

There was a roar from the crowd, followed by a hush and Ron felt the world begin to tilt. He gripped the necklace the girl had given him and felt himself rolling. He jumped toward the crowd that had opened for the first time since Ron had entered it.

Ron landed on his feet, staggered and sat down. He turned in time to see the float list slowly, irrevocably, with people leaping off and away from it. It landed on its side, losing a little crêpe paper, and the people closed back around it, jumping up and down, chanting and screaming. Someone pulled Ron to his feet and kissed him, shouting something about the captain and his ship. He tried to return the embrace but he stumbled against a wall of people. The laughing crowd shouted and shoved at him and Ron liked to have their hands on him like that. It wasn't a mean shoving, but something that friends might do.

Ron closed his eyes and sniffed at the perfume the kiss had left near his face. He started to dance with himself, but someone soft slipped under his arms and they danced together, to the music seeping out of a bar. Ron never opened his eyes and when the song was over his partner kissed him hard on the mouth and spun off into the crowd. Ron wondered if it could have been his wife. They had used to dance slowly like that together, in their living room, before the girls were old enough to tease them.

Ron stumbled on and realized he had fallen out of the thickest part of the crowd. He turned a corner, looking for it again, and then another one. But the party had lost him. He could almost walk now, but it was hard to stand up without the support of the crowd.

He crossed a large cobblestoned square. He sat down once, un-expectedly, and traced the joints between the bricks with his fingers. There were a lot of people here, he realized, looking at all the moving legs. But not like before. He could see past these legs. They didn't block out everything else.

He stood and continued his crossing. At the other end of the square, past its wrought-iron fencing, was a café of some sort, brightly lit with colorful awnings. Ron steered away from it and sidled along a large dark building, edging farther and farther out of the protection of the crowd.

Ron stopped at the huge log pilings. There were still fireworks bursting over his head and he watched them reflecting in the rolling surface of the big river. It was no longer muddy. The water sparkled and shined and flowered in the colorful bursts of the rockets. Yet it flowed as same as ever, and Ron knew it never once wrapped its legs around strangers. Even though it could change from muddy and drab to this colorful, quiet splendor, Ron knew it would never do that.

He stumbled to the ladder-like stairway that led strangely right into the river. He walked slowly down the iron steps and felt the warm water close around his ankles. He took another step but there were no more on the stairway and Ron plunged into the river.

The surprising current took him away from the ladder immediately and Ron rolled onto his back and watched an enormous burst of color open up above him. He smiled. His ears were under the water and he could not hear the explosion. Ron let his body relax into the nudging flow of the river and he wished that everything had always stayed like this. Then he had the odd thought that maybe they had and that the naked stranger was simply one of those quick bursts of riotousness that flashed onto the river now and then, leaving it unchanged when it faded.

He turned over then and started to swim down the stream, quietly so he didn't disturb the surface. His ears were out of the water and the noise returned to him but he no longer had to watch the bright violent flashes of the fireworks.

There was a row of small, white lights looping from a stick framework on the left bank of the river and Ron could see people standing under them. One of them pointed and soon they were yelling at him and Ron dove under the surface. When he came up a few feet later there was more yelling and laughing and some cursing. A boat motor started and Ron told the man in it that he wanted to stay out here but was soon dragged back to shore. The man was a waiter and he was mad but laughing, and he brought Ron a free cup of coffee because he never saw a first at Mardi Gras anymore.

People crowded around Ron's table and laughed at him and wanted to know what he was doing. He told them he was swimming to Denver to a woman who was his wife. They laughed so hard one of them fell over and Ron looked at him on the floor and he started to smile too.

He told them he had been cheated by the quietest thing he had ever known, but that if it could be quiet again he thought he would go back. They cheered. It was a long, long drive though, and Ron stood back up and wandered away from the river, toward where the roar was most tumultuous. It was probably equally chaotic in his house in Denver right now, and he thought it wouldn't hurt for that to continue for a while yet.

When he did call Denver the sky was beginning to lighten and he had considerable trouble talking. He told her he was at the Mardi Gras and that it had been great fun and he wished she had come with him. She was crying hard and he looked down the street, at the colored men who were already beginning to hose down the cobblestone and then he looked up to the iron balconies where no naked women hung.

His wife began to speak but Ron interrupted her and said again what a great, crowded party it had been but that it was over now, wasn't it, and he thought he would come home.

The Tall Uncut

When she first came to rescue me I was young enough that after a while I thought I'd always lived with her. Even then—I must've been all of two or three—she looked that wrinkled up. She has a face like one of those heads you see somebody's made out of an apple. Wizened'd be the word, I guess, if you ever used words like that. Looks like all the flesh has slowly been taken out of her. But I always thought she was so strong. Like she'd taken everything thrown at her and was still standing. Not like she'd ever have to build her whole life out of lies.

Strong as she was, one of the first memories I have of her, after coming to live with her in her house in Chicago, was of waking up one night and being scared and walking through the strange house getting more and more scared and being drawn to the single light in the kitchen. Like a moth. She was just sitting there crying at the table, with the paper napkin holder and the salt and the pepper shakers shaped like Mt. Rushmore. That wasn't what I expected to find in the middle of the night and I guess I started crying too. She drew me up into that lap of hers and pressed my head into the soft parts of her chest and we sat there at the table crying.

Back when we still talked to each other, if that night ever came up she'd swear that I kept saying, "It'll be all right, Grandma. It'll be all right." I'm not sure I ever did believe that though.

That was pretty soon after the accident. We didn't do that again, and I think if she cried anymore after that, she was careful to keep it away from me. Her daughter, my mom, was flying the plane when it went in over the Black Hills. My dad was with her. I was at the babysitter's. It was hard on me of course, but with the kind of foggy way death hits when you're little. I believed Grandma when she told me I'd see Mommy and Daddy later in heaven. For a long time I asked her if we could go to heaven yet, to see them. Later I'd have whole guilty days remembering how I kept bringing it up. She said her husband, my grandpa, had gone down in a plane too. Shot down by the Japanese while flying freight into the Chinese during some part of the war. And I believed that too. I didn't have any reason not to.

That had happened a long, long time before I was born, so I didn't miss my grandpa either. But I heard more about him than I did about my own parents. He was practically all she talked about, and he always seemed to get better and better. She said he was a logger before he was a pilot and that before she'd become a teacher they had logged together, all through the depression, which she made sound a lot more hopeful than it'd seem. That was up north, in the top end of Wisconsin—what Grandma still called the Tall Uncut. My grandma took me on one vacation and that's where we went. I was afraid of the Peshtigo fire for months, after seeing paintings of the people sitting in the river with the flames all through the night around them. Then Grandma told me all of Chicago had burned down the same time as Peshtigo. That was all a hundred years ago, she said, to try to calm me down, but it didn't do much. Big numbers didn't mean much to me. Whenever I asked her how old she was she always said a hundred and twenty-seven. I don't know why she said things like that.

Grandma said my grandpa learned to fly as soon as she picked up her teaching job. She had a thing about flying though, and she never talked about it much. And she never did say how she went from logging camps to teaching. She made more money than he ever had with the logs though, so they moved down to Chicago and had a baby. She said he'd been flying mail and some freight when he left for China. Grandma never said what drew him way to hell over there. Could've got drafted I guess, but that was never the idea I had of it. As I got older I saw that almost every story Grandma told had holes big enough to pitch cats through.

After Grandpa was gone she was left with just my mom, who was only three then. She was eighteen when my dad found her. He was on a trip through Chicago on business, and he took her back out to Rapid City, or Rapid as Grandma said he called it, like there wasn't enough time in the world.

He was just some kind of salesman and as I was growing up I pictured Grandma watching her daughter leave with him. Here Grandpa had been a logger up in The Tall Uncut, and then a pilot flying The Hump over the Himalayas, dodging flak and Jap Zeros and everything. And his daughter gets hooked by some travelling salesman with a briefcase. I held that against my dad, who without pictures I wouldn't have remembered at all.

Even as a bone-headed ten-year-old I could see how Grandma's face looked when she talked about the Tall Uncut. Later she transferred it to mean everything west of the Mississippi. She still meant it to mean wildness and virgin country I guess, like the loggers had. But whenever she used Tall Uncut to mean the West, where she lost her daughter and then me, she didn't have the look she had when she talked about her young, starting-out years, when the Tall Uncut meant the big timber and her husband up in it and her cooking at the log camps, with everything around them so big and new that they felt they could do anything and nothing would ever stop them.

Whenever she used to write, after I'd gone out to Rapid myself, where those salt and pepper shakers had come from, she'd start with, "How are things out in the Tall Uncut?" It always made me feel uncomfortable, like I should move up to Peshtigo or someplace like that. I was also finding out some of the truth by then and I was starting to feel like everything she'd ever said came out of a fog, and that all the roots I had in the world were just made up. It made me feel like an orphan, which was something I'd never felt like before.

I drifted a little after high school, like most kids, but even less anchored to anything. I pulled up in Rapid to see what it was like. Pretty soon I was logging myself, working a saw for one of the big timber corporations, and during the off time I started reading up on the old-time loggers. I got started on that because I just couldn't believe anybody'd ever really cut down more than a tree or two before they had chainsaws. I hardly believed anything anymore, and maybe all I was really doing was checking up on Grandma.

I was pretty startled to read the Tall Uncut was nothing but a memory by the 1890s—fifteen years before Grandma was born. No logging camps after that, no great stands of white pine bigger around than a house. Nothing but sand and slash.

There was no Tall Uncut left.

At first I didn't believe the books I was reading. I wrote to some of the towns Grandma had mentioned when she'd get a little misty about the Uncut—to historical societies and places like that. None of them had ever heard of Grandpa though. A few knew about some old loggers, or young ones trying to carry it on, that'd roved the old, torn-out woods, living in their trucks, finding just enough wood to get by. One of them even sent a faded photo of some poor old ghost, bringing in the last of the old pines. A one-log load. The letter said they still didn't know how he had cut it and brought it in, since it must have been way back where it had been missed and there was only the one man in the picture. It wasn't Grandpa of course, but I figured he could have done it. I was proud of him and felt awful at the same time.

I remembered the stories Grandma'd told of cooking in the big camps, and all the big, tired men with their crushes on her, and I wondered why she ever said anything like that. I pictured her over a camp fire in some slash pile, alone, cooking up whatever they could afford. How she got a teaching job from that I still couldn't figure. I wrote more letters, and not one old mill or lumber yard or historical society had ever heard of either of them. I started wondering if she'd ever been up there at all.

It was the only way I'd ever heard of my grandpa though, so I built a frame for that picture and set it on the dresser in my bedroom. I put it away whenever Grandma visited. I didn't tell her what I knew about the Uncut.

I don't know what got my mom into flying. Grandma's only comment was that our family never was meant for the air and it nearly killed her when she found out my mom was learning. I wondered what she'd told her about Grandpa. That might have had something to do with it, who knows?

But I'd guess it was boredom mostly. Rapid couldn't've been much after Chicago, even though she'd left there at eighteen. I think she took the lessons while my dad was on the road. I know she was flying solo before I was born. She was only twenty when she had me. She flew my dad on his longer business trips and they spent a lot more time together that way. After I was a year old she started again, leaving me with a neighbor for up to a week at a time while she flew around with my dad.

She got into trouble one time for buzzing Mount Rushmore. Grandma told me about it once, and I looked that up too. That, at least, was true. It made the Rapid papers back in 1960. They weren't nearly as thrilled with it as I was. She must have been in the first month of her pregnancy. Probably didn't even know that then, but once I found out I liked to suppose it was a celebration stunt, like a victory roll.

The more I checked up on her, the less and less I saw Grandma. It wasn't as easy anymore, with the travel and all. And I'd quit making the effort. By this time I'd seen things like her diploma from the Chicago Normal School, where they trained the teachers, and her and Grandpa's marriage license, and his army record. I didn't much like getting lied to as an adult. As a kid, when I'd've believed anything just to have some sort of family, it seemed a lot worse.

After a while I got into flying myself, but I didn't do it out of boredom so much. I was still just sawing and I was married by then and living in a trailer, with a kid on the way, which turned out to be twins, and working like a dog eight months of the year and sitting around going crazy the other four.

I saw a show on TV about helicopter logging, and I knew right away that the money was in the air. And in some stupid way I figured it'd be getting back at Grandma for making up my whole life as a kid.

I did fixed wing, just to get the license, then went straight to helicopters. I did it in the winters, when I wasn't sawing, but it took a lot of money and it required a little faith from Gina, my wife. It took three years and I worried so much about it being a strain on us I damn near made it one. By the time I had enough hours to start flying for the logging outfits we'd been on the ropes for a while. But we had to move to Washington, where they fly out the big logs, and leaving that trailer at the edge of the Badlands was the biggest thing we'd ever done.

I didn't mind at all that I'd left Grandma that much farther behind.

So I started flying logs out of the real Tall Uncut and earning an amount of money I just couldn't believe. Work wasn't so damn exhausting anymore and pretty soon we started taking vacations when I was down.

When we took the vacation to Chicago, because the boys kept pestering and I never had told Gina why I'd lost my interest in Grandma, I had to take the whole group aside and let them in on the secret. I told them I was working on a giant surprise for Grandma, one that we couldn't let her in on, no way, until it was ready, or it would be ruined forever. I let them know that the biggest part of the surprise was that I was a pilot now, and that they mustn't, mustn't, mustn't let her know that.

I'd always figured being a pilot would be something I could throw in her face, to show her how much I thought of everything she'd ever said. If I hadn't read the investigation of my folks' accident I wouldn't have believed that either. But when it came right down to it, I was scared to let her know.

I hinted at things, flying and bringing Grandma to the coast to live—she was a favorite then with the boys—and Robbie, the sensitive one, got so worried it would fall apart he started to cry on the drive to Chicago. I even tried to pull this wool over Gina's eyes. But the first night back in Grandma's house, with the boys tucked in and Grandma herself back in her room, Gina and I were lying in the fold-out couch in the living room when right out of the blue Gina said, "When are you going to tell her?"

I played stupid for a second, but I was embarrassed I thought Gina would fall for the same trick I was using on our six-year-olds. "Never," I said. "Never. She couldn't take it." Really all I wanted was to avoid a fight with Grandma. I get carried away in fights and I knew I'd lose no matter what happened.

Gina was never one for secrecy, but I put my foot down. I got cranky and I didn't tell her all I should've, to let her know why. What happened between me and Grandma was none of her business I figured.

So we spent the week and the kids loved it and after a while I stopped trying to pick apart everything she said. At the end of the week I figured Grandma was none the wiser, and we all promised to visit as soon as we got another chance. Then, while Gina was loading the boys into the car and I was inside checking to make sure we hadn't left anything, Grandma grabbed hold of my arm. I hadn't known she was there and she startled me.

"Quit your flying right now," she hissed. "Didn't I tell you about the flying?" She was trying to be quiet, so the boys wouldn't hear. She sounded like a snake. She shook my arm when I didn't answer. "Didn't I tell you?"

Just the way she did it, like I was getting a spanking, set me off. I stared at her. "You told me a lot of things, Grandma," I said.

"Well, you better start listening."

"Oh, I listened all right." I had to pull her fingers off my arm. "I listened all the time. I even believed it for a while."

I was aiming to hurt and even through all those wrinkles I could see I'd hit the mark. "I don't know what you're talking about," she said, but there wasn't any snake left in her.

I kept on anyway, still feeling where her fingers had clutched at me. "You and all your Uncut baloney, that's what I mean. I can read, Grandma. You guys weren't ever up there." She was hurt and why I didn't stop I don't know.

"You started teaching here right out of Chicago Normal, same time as you got married. I even saw your marriage license."

At first she'd looked like I was letting her air out, but then she flared back. She actually slapped me, hissing again, and calling me an ungrateful wretch.

That's when I let her have it. I said, "And Grandpa never went to China either. He went AWOL from flight school. The army's still got the case open. He just flat ass left you. Didn't he?"

She was trembling by then and so was I. Grandpa was all I'd ever had, and even after I'd found out, I'd tried to forget what I'd learned. I'd cut the feet out from under both of us.

Grandma wasn't hissing anymore, but shouting. Shouting, "Get out of this house! Get out of this house forever!"

I turned and saw Gina there, but she turned in front of me and we got in the wagon together and drove away. I was still trembling when I stopped to gas up and Gina jumped out and closed the door so the boys wouldn't hear.

"What in the world?" she wanted to know.

"She found out I was flying," I said. I was already feeling what a son of a bitch I'd been and I never allowed that visit to be mentioned again.

So I went back to lifting logs out of the Uncut and I didn't hear from her again. I kind of waited for her to call, but years went by with nothing. I figured, even though she'd lied like she had, that I was the one that needed forgiving, and that's not easy to make the first move on. Her lies really were harmless enough; I'd just gotten pissed that I'd been fooled for so long. So I kept waiting, hoping she'd come through. But as more time passed I began to suspect that the call I'd get would be the one announcing a broken hip or a stroke, or maybe just a finishing heart attack. I never would've guessed it'd happen the other way around.

I'd been working long enough in the air by then that it wasn't scary anymore. But swinging a helicopter around above the timber, and pulling logs off the steep stuff with a two-hundred-foot cable is not something you can ever daydream over.

I had a new guy in as my co-pilot and I'd decided he was an asshole. That's not easy to say now, but I'd just bought an interest in the helicopter I flew, which was pretty much unheard of, but would increase my profit if things went well, and right off this new guy started telling me what a mistake I'd made. We were way back in hock again and I didn't much need to hear about it. I was worrying on that when I should've been flying.

We were lifting a load off and it got tangled in some slash that was stuck into some of the big stuff that wasn't down yet and I felt the helicopter bog some and knew what was happening. I didn't want to release the load because the choker setter was down there and he sure didn't need all that crashing down on him. I'd just started trying to bull it out some when the new guy reminds me about the winds, which were doing some ugly gusting. But I didn't need to be reminded by him. I was pulling full power and starting to pendulum a touch when the wind hit and on his own the new guy pops the load release, which only made it worse. The wind already had us sideways and I didn't have a prayer of controlling anything.

This all happened a lot quicker than I can tell.

The new guy just stared at me. I could see that but I was in the last instant of thinking there was anything I could do and it didn't really register until a long time later. I wagged the stick once, then I remember switching everything off, thinking I'd just wait for it to go in. I was already on the high side, which was the best chance I had. I wasn't up much though, and there was no wait.

The rotors touched first, by fractions of a second, and there were a couple of shots as they broke apart. I remember, even with no time left at all, and all hell breaking loose everywhere, that the sound of those rotors going startled me, like backfires on a quiet street.

The transmission, still wound up and flying, tore loose when we hit. It came through the cockpit and took out the co-pilot, though I didn't know any of this until the reports started being worked on.

I broke both my legs bad. The cockpit kind of folded around them and I had to be cut out. They're held together now with pins and plates and all that, and I don't believe walking will ever be what it used to be. But there wasn't any fire, not a lick of it. Of course there wouldn't have been a lick. Any lick would've turned into great, slothering tongues and I'd've died screaming.

When I was still under the drugs and the pain, I woke and Grandma was the first person I saw. I wasn't sure she was real, but we had long talks and it was like being a kid again, with me scared and her strong, and now I can't remember a single word of any of it.

The first time I can remember still, when my head had cleared, I woke with Gina kissing me on the forehead, telling me Grandma was here and she'd be back herself in a little while.

I saw Grandma standing there after Gina left. She didn't sit down, but looked at me, until she was sure I was finally back and in my senses. Then she said, "So you're still out levelling the last of the Uncut." Like we'd never had a rough word between us in our lives.

I could see she was trying to make light of it and I tried to smile myself and then I saw the tears winding down that wrinkled face.

She said, "Shame on you. Not my old Uncut."

But then her voice failed her and she turned away. "Not flying," she murmured, "not the slippery, slippery, murderous air." She walked out of the room then and didn't come back. When Gina returned I asked if Grandma was here, in town, and Gina laughed and said something about the drugs they were giving me.

But I was serious and I asked again. "Of course she is," Gina told me. "She just went home. She was out in the hall when I came in. She said you were sleeping."

Once I was out of the bed and into the wheelchair and then finally home, which did not happen over night, Grandma was all moved into my new house at the edge of the mountains. She told me that the lack of flames in my crash was the one solid piece of evidence she had proving there's a heaven. She said my mom was doing that, blowing out any flame before it could start. She was shaking when she said it, trembling, and I didn't say anything. My mom and dad's plane had burned.

We never did talk about anything that mattered and when I was finally up using a walker some, Grandma decided I'd pull through and she packed her bags one night and said she was ready to leave. She'd bussed the whole way out, rather than fly, but we talked her out of taking the bus again and decided Gina'd take her back with the kids and make a vacation out of it. They'd all missed her.

They wanted to hire a nurse to stay with me full time, but for Christsakes, I'm not a cripple, and I settled for one checking on me in the afternoons.

On the day they left Grandma came into my room, where Gina was saying goodbye to me. She was done up for the trip and Gina said, "You look like a million bucks, Grandma."

She was fiddling with something on my dresser, and when she turned I saw that it was my old picture of the logger with the last of the Tall Uncut loaded onto his truck. She smiled at my wife, but said, "I've looked like this for fifty years," which really wasn't much of an exaggeration.

I said, "That'd be since you were seventy-seven then." It was her smallest lie, and I don't know why I brought it up at all.

She knew right away what I meant and she smiled a little. But then she said, "It's flying that did this to me. Sometimes I think I aged so fast God hasn't realized how old I really am. That's the only reason I'm still around."

Gina said something appropriate, like "Don't talk so," but Grandma waved it off. I saw that she had turned that old picture face down on the dresser.

"I'm ready to go," she said. She was looking right at me, where I sat, still stove up in bed. "I'm not going to want to see you die. No one should have to see their children die."

I looked away for a second. She only had the one child, my mom, but over the years, without them, she kind of adopted my dad, as well as me. I think she even included Grandpa in the list of children she'd seen die. Being left like that must've been as bad.

I looked back up and she was smiling again. She waved her hand in front of her face, and said, "It really will be good to see them all again." She said it like it would all be a pleasant little visit.

Grandma crossed the room then and kissed me on the forehead, like she had since I was two or three. "I'd have gone a long time ago, you know," she said, and she winked, "But I'm afraid of the flight."

Then she leaned in even closer and whispered, "I had to have something to tell your mother. It was all she had left. The Tall Uncut was just a bedtime story. That's all. It was that or lose everything."

She looked at me but I was looking at the sheet rising and falling over my chest. "But I've lost everything anyway, haven't I?" she said. "So it is all I have left."

She stood up and patted my arm and I said, thanks for coming out, or something idiotic like that, and she left.

I lay there in bed all day, the house ringing with the quiet. I hurt and I wondered what I had done.

When the nurse came that afternoon I had her give me some pain killers. Then I asked her to flip that picture of the Uncut right side up. I introduced her to my Grandpa.